Tranquility

A novel

By Tim Easley

For those who make the seconds count and
my father for giving a helping hand.

RYAN

    I've made mistakes. I always owned up to them. I never took the easy way out. I kept it together. She would have wanted that. Which is easier said than done. The days just melt. The nights are lonely. You can get used to a lot of things. You never get used to being by yourself. I'm no one special; I was going out exactly the way I came in.

    Alone.

    Helen was my rock. She made my days worth living. When I lost her to cancer five years ago, it broke me. There is no other way to describe it. Her death decimated the illusions I had about life. I thought we were going to be old together. Watch the grandkids grow. Fate had other plans.

    Helen was strong, that much was certain. She fought the cancer every step of the way with a dignity that most wished they could have in life. When it became clear to her she wasn't going to beat it, she was at peace. Helen didn't get mad. She was more concerned about me. Helen knew she was the glue. She knew that I would fall apart.

    She was right.

    Two nights before she died, Helen spoke to me. I was by her side, a place I rarely left anymore. Visiting hours certainly did not apply to me.

    I held her hand. Her skin was rough like sand paper. The chemo had affected in her in other ways, but this was the one I noticed the most. Her skin used to be smooth like lace. I would shiver at her touch.

"Ryan," she said her voice hoarse.

"I'm here Helen. I'm here," I said.

"I need you to do something for me."

"Anything you need sweetheart."

"I need you to live," she said, sputtering a loud, hacking cough.

"I don't understand," I said.

"Yes, you do," Helen replied, gripping my hand tighter. "I'm not going to be here much longer."

The air in my lungs caught as I processed what she said. I had never wanted to consider the option. Helen was going to pull through like she always did, and yet there she was, saying the words I couldn't comprehend.

"Don't say that honey," I said my voice cracking as I tried not to cry. "You're going to be just fine."

"Liar," she said smiling.

I kissed her. I wanted to hold that moment forever.

"You need to pull it together, dear," Helen said her voice tinged with sorrow. "Daniel is going to need you."

I couldn't hold it in anymore. I held her and cried. It wasn't supposed to end like this. Not like this.

Helen, the saint she was, wiped away my tears as if I was a small child. She always knew what to do. What to say.

"I'll miss you," she said.

My wife died peacefully in her sleep on a Saturday afternoon. I had stepped out for only a moment to get coffee when she passed. When I saw the rush of doctors and nurses run into her room, I knew the worst had become reality. By the time I got in there, it was too late. She was gone. She had died alone and I did not get to say goodbye.

I will always hate myself for that.

The funeral was awful which is a stupid thing to say. Of course it was awful. You would think for the worst day of my life, the weather could at least be decent. Apparently, God didn't get to my request.

It rained the entire time. Not a misting, but a full on torrential downpour. Everyone had brought umbrellas but they did little good. Within minutes we were soaked to the bone. The rain kept me numb, which was good. I didn't want to feel anything. I wasn't sure what I would do if I did.

It was a small gathering, only about twenty people. Helen and I had only a few friends, but it wasn't an issue with us. It was better to have a select group. Ones we could depend on when the chips were down. I was glad to have them on that day.

Daniel's reaction was more or less what mine would have been if I been able to let go. He was our only child and he loved his mother dearly. He cried openly. His wife, Meredith, did her best to put on a brave face for the family.

Kayla, my granddaughter, was two at the time. She sat in a fold out chair as the service concluded. She fidgeted a bit as any small child would but to her credit, she spoke nary a word during the whole thing. She was well behaved; Daniel and Meredith were raising her right.

When it came time for me to say a few words, I couldn't do it. The words would not come to me. I couldn't articulate them. The sadness of her being taken from me hindered my attempts. I stood there, flustering and mumbling on what was supposed to be an eloquent eulogy for my dearly departed Helen.

Daniel could sense something was wrong. He walked away from Meredith and asked if I was okay. Obviously, a dumb question to ask, but I knew what he meant. In that moment I let go and wept. Daniel grabbed my arm and pulled me away. For the second time, I did not get to finish saying goodbye.

The reception was no better. It was if all color had drained. I could only see grey. The guests spoke in hushed tones as they munched on crackers and carrot sticks. They would come up to me to give their condolences. I shook their hands and nodded my thanks. None of it mattered though. It all felt hollow.

They meant what they said, that much I knew, but it didn't feel right. I could remember the wakes I attended for friends who had lost someone, I'd shake their hands and say how sorry I was. Problem was you feel true grief only when it directly affects you. Sometimes you don't feel it even when it does. You notice a void, but life goes on. For the moment you remain and nothing matters.

I saw my son talking to his wife. He seemed better now. I needed to speak to him. I walked across the room and stood next to him.

"Son," I said. It was the only thing I could think of.

"Dad," he replied back.

"Can we talk for a minute?"

"Sure."

We moved upstairs to the master bedroom. I shut the door slowly, hearing an audible creak. I made a mental note to get some oil to fix it.

"What did you want to talk about?" Daniel asked.

"I wanted to make sure you were okay," I said.

"I'm okay," Daniel said, pacing the room. "How are you holding up?"

I faked a smile. It was harder than I imagined.

"I'm going to be fine," I said, not believing my own voice.

"Are you sure?" he asked me, his face showing worry. Daniel was a good son. He always put others before himself. It was admirable. He got that from his mother, rest her soul.

"Positive," I lied.

I hugged my son. I wanted him to believe everything was okay. I wanted to convince myself.

"I'm glad we talked," Daniel said relieved. "I was worried about you."

"No need to be," I said.

I failed her. I broke my promise. I never thought I'd do it, but I did. Some things are too painful to overcome. I wish I could say it was a slow process but I'd be lying.

Within weeks of her passing, I cut myself off from the world. I stopped spending time with our friends. I gave them no explanation, no justification. I just let them go. I surrounded myself in solitude. I likened myself to Thoreau, the man who went to live with nature and become one with it. I was a fool, and I was being selfish. I didn't care. I wanted my Helen back, and was doing everything short of pulling the trigger to end it.

The relationship with my son was the largest casualty of this change. Daniel would call the house, and I'd respond with curt responses. He would come over and I would pretend I wasn't home. When that wasn't possible, I'd force him to go away. I had shut myself off. If it meant losing him too, so be it. My heart ached when I thought of him, but I ignored it. I wasn't thinking straight anymore.

Daniel stop coming by; stopped calling too. I can only imagine it broke his heart. In my delusional state, it had to be done. He had his own family to take care of. Daniel didn't need to be part of my mess.

To make my days pass, I spent them tinkering with broken things. There were plenty to fix. My house was old and barely holding together even with my constant vigilance. That could only keep me content for so long. I grew restless. Though I wasn't keen on rejoining the world, I thought it was necessary to acquire a companion before I went mad. I got a dog, a golden lab I named Robert. He was chipper and full of energy. He became my closest friend in no time.

That became my routine. I'd wake up early and have a light breakfast. Robert would bark and wag his tail. I'd grab his leash and take him on walks. It was the closest I got to being part of the world. After that, I'd send him outside while I toyed with the latest challenge my workshop could provide. I'd eat sparse lunches then retire to the study to read.

After dinner, Robert and I would retire to the den and watch television. It wasn't complex, but it was what I liked. Robert didn't mind either. On the other hand, being that Robert was a dog, he would like anything as long as he continued to be spoiled. I had found my way to cope. To live, like Helen wanted. Maybe I hadn't broken my promise after all.

Then that goddamn message had to flash across the screen and ruin it all.

It was a Thursday evening. We were in the living room for our evening television. Robert was grumpy and I ignored it. There wasn't anything on TV. I switched over to CNN. I could be informed at least.

The broadcaster was blabbing away about a crisis in the Middle East as if it was something new. My mind turned off just listening to him. My attention span is not what it used to be. Robert barking loudly snapped me out of my trance. Robert didn't care for news. He sometimes forgot that it wasn't a democracy, but a dictatorship in this house, and he wasn't Hugo Chavez in the equation.

"Quiet!" I barked back. Robert held his head down and whimpered more.

And that's when it happened. There was some static in the picture, that black and white snow that shows up when you punch in a channel that doesn't exist. It was just a bit at first and I ignored it, thinking the TV was going bad. Then it encompassed the entire screen. I began to worry. I pushed my recliner into the forward position and went over to take a look. I checked all the wiring and nothing seemed to be amiss. It puzzled me.

The screen changed again to a bright white picture accompanied with a loud shrill beeping noise. I lowered the volume. Audio wasn't necessary for whatever was going on. A short statement, comprised of just two sentences appeared on the screen with bold lettering and in all caps.

The World Shall End In Three Days Time. Be Prepared.

The first thing that went through my mind was this was some sick joke. There were plenty of nut jobs who "claimed" to know when the world would end. The Mayans were an old standby. Harold Camping and the May 21st group was the laughingstock of the nation for about two weeks. Those who claimed to know were derided as foolish and quickly discredited as such. I knew the feed would return and within the hour, the news would report this was nothing more than a prank. The perpetrator would be revealed to be a twelve year old hacker who thought it would be funny to scare mommy and daddy. No more, no less.

That made me the king of wishful thinking.

"This is Jonathan Quinlan at CNN. We interrupt our regularly scheduled broadcast for this breaking news announcement. At exactly 10:56 p.m. Eastern Standard Time, a rogue video feed hijacked all forms of technological communication globally to deliver a short but chilling message. It read: The World Shall End In Three Days Time. Be Prepared.

This should be the point of the story where we explain that it was all a ruse, and the perpetrator has already been caught. Things have turned out to be much more complex than initially thought. This message was apparently only part of what was to be sent. Only ten minutes ago, CNN Headquarters received a computer file that detailed scientific readings, complex mathematical calculations and other pertinent information. Information that gives potential credence to this alleged doomsday warning.

We have unconfirmed reports that the heads of state across the globe have received this information as well, though no country has given an official confirmation. Sources at the White House say the President will speak to the nation within the hour. CNN will keep you up to date on the latest breaking developments. We will return shortly after this commercial break.

The President came on the air. He gave a brave face, stressing the information was just in preliminary rounds of analysis. He said the nation should not fall into hysteria. I read between the lines. The guy looked like he had several Jack and Cokes, minus the Coke. His voice was calm but the eyes told a different story. No one pays attention to the eyes. I do, for the eyes are the gateway to truth. His eyes told me two things; this was real and he was worried.

The first thing that flashed through my mind was Daniel. Despite everything I had put him through, he was still my son. I wanted to hear his voice. He seemed to have the same idea. The phone rang and I picked up.
"Hello," I said.
"Is that you Dad?" Daniel asked.
"I'm here son."
"Christ Dad, what the hell is going on? This message splashes across the screen then the President is on TV telling us not to worry. You know the rule about when they tell you not to panic. "
"That's when you run," I said
"Meredith is worried," Daniel said.
"I could understand that," I replied grimly.
"What are you going to do?" Daniel asked.

The question gave me pause. I'm not particularly young at sixty eight, but I took care of myself. I still had plenty of lead left in the pencil. The question of the world ending is one jested over coffee. It's a "what if" for a reason; it's something that is never actually supposed to happen. Now the "if" may have become a reality.

"Earth to Dad," Daniel called out.

I shook my head to reorient myself.

"Sorry," I said, "Got lost in my thoughts."

"You should visit. We'd love to have you."

He was trying to be nice. Daniel didn't hate me but he was disappointed in how I've acted. I couldn't blame him. If we met face to face, I'm not sure what would happen. Would we have anything to say to each other?

"I don't think that's best," I said.

"Dad—"Daniel began.

"I'm going to the cabin."

I was referring to the family cabin thirty miles outside of the city, deep in the woods. It had been in the family for generations. I loved it immensely and I had many a good memory there. I asked Helen to marry me in those woods. Daniel was conceived there.

The cabin had everything I needed and nothing to distract me. It had electricity and water, but that was it. There was no phone or cable to make the mind idle. It would just be me, Robert, and nature together to the end.

"That dilapidated shack in the woods," Daniel scoffed. "Are you serious Dad?"

"Dead serious," I said.

"You should spend time with your family. That's what I'd do."

"I'm not you, son."

"Dad," Daniel said, irritation creeping into his voice. "You are being irrational. Not to mention selfish."

"I need you to understand."

He hung up on me.

He was right though. I was being irrational, but there was nothing rational about what was happening. The world might end in three days. I could imagine how people were going to handle that. Answer being, not well. There was going to mass panic, and above all else there could be violence. I wanted to avoid it entirely. Have my modicum of peace. I looked down to Robert. He was no longer grumpy. He was at fully alert, his tail whipping back and forth so quick I thought it might actually break off. I patted his head and headed for the bedroom.

"Come on boy," I said. "We have packing to do."

I considered leaving in the morning, but thought better of it. The longer this was out, the worse it would get. I didn't want to be in the middle of it. I wanted to be tucked away, so I began to pack.

I grabbed a military duffel bag for I was packing light. The cabin had almost everything I needed; fresh linens, canned food for Robert and me, and a good book or two. I did require some clothes so I snatched them quickly, stuffing them into my bag. In addition, I grabbed a few mementos; a necklace Helen always wore, the last photo the three of us took together as a family, and my father's pocketknife.

There was one more thing to get, rather two things. I descended into the basement, my worn boots making loud noises as they hit the stairs. My hands touched the cool metal of the safe and I spun the combination from memory.

I reached inside and pulled out two guns. The first was a 1911 .45 caliber pistol that had been handed down in the family. When I die, it would have been passed on to my son. The second was a .308 Savage 99 rifle that I used for hunting. I took several boxes of ammo for each. I didn't think I'd need them, but it would be foolish not to have them.

Traffic was horrendous. Everyone and their mother were attempting to get away. Their destination was anybody's guess. It wasn't like anyone could escape it. The end of world meant exactly that; nothing would be left. I concentrated on the road. I had ten miles to go, and I focused on that.

It took almost six hours to travel those ten miles. The sun was starting to peak through the dark sky. The second I could turn, I twisted the wheel right and sped away from the madness. Another mile and a half and I would be in walking distance of my cabin.

Fate, the crafty devil it is, decided to mess with me further. The car engine began to click and clack, sputtering to a halt. So close and yet so far I thought. I jumped out of the driver seat and went to unlatch the hood and see what the problem was. A cloud of black smoke billowed out. The piece of shit was shot. Even if I could fix it, it would take hours. Time I did not have.

I whistled for Robert to jump out of the car while I opened the trunk and retrieved my duffel. I slung it over my shoulder. I kicked the clunker formerly known as my car for good measure, and I began to walk, Robert following close behind. With any luck I could make it before the sun fully came up.

We made it just as the woods began to come alive. Robert and I were exhausted. We both needed shut eye. I remained on my toes, cautious against potential danger. Five minutes more wasn't worth sleeping for good before my time. I surveyed the property to make sure there were no surprises for us. When I was satisfied, I opened the door and let the air invigorate my stuffy abode. I headed for the kitchen to pour Robert chow. I knew he was hungry. As he chomped away, I quickly consumed a breakfast bar. I could deal with hunger, what I needed was rest.

I woke up to the sound of Robert barking in the kitchen. My body was sore. I rubbed my eyes and glanced at the clock. It was past four in the afternoon.

"Goddamn," I swore to myself. I hadn't intended to sleep that long. I wanted as much time awake as I could have. I could sleep when I was dead.

I pulled myself out of bed and stretched, setting my back into place with an audible pop. I grimaced as my joints creaked. I entered the den and found Robert splayed out on the floor. Ironically, it was his turn to nap. I shook my head and sighed.

"So what should we have for dinner, boy?" I spoke in a hush tone, not wanting to wake him. I reached for my coat. "How does venison sound? It sounds good to me."

Most people don't understand hunting. It is a patient man's sport and most city folk aren't. It takes a certain type to move through the forest with no guarantee of success. It's like gambling, it isn't about winning or losing; it's about the game.

I had been traipsing through the woods with little success. My intuition told me that if I just gave it a little more, the day would not be for naught. Sure enough, fifteen minutes later an eight point buck walked into a clearing thirty feet from where I was. The trek was going to be worth it after all. I slowly pulled the rifle off my shoulder and aimed methodically through my scope.

My finger slowly applied pressure to the trigger when something else came into view. The buck was not alone. He was joined by several other does that nibbled at the ground around him. The gun in my hand got a lot heavier and the trigger became immobile.

I couldn't do it. It shouldn't of matter; they weren't people and no one would care that I killed that deer, but I cared. It was a reminder of what was about to be lost. What I lost.

I placed my eye back to the scope and tilted the rifle upward. I aimed for a tree not far from where they stood and pulled the trigger. The shot cracked in the quiet forest and they all scampered off to unknown parts. I returned the rifle to my shoulder and started walking back, the light wind chilling me.

I had chicken soup that night. Robert had more dog food, but he didn't care. Food was food. It was starting to get nippy outside so I collected kindling to start a fire. In a few minutes the cabin was basked in heat from the fire and I started to feel better.

Robert decided to retire for the evening and found his place in his bedding near the bathroom. I had no intention of doing that yet. There wasn't much else to do though so I flipped through family photos. I found a book that had the three of us together. It felt like yesterday.

Daniel never cared for camping. I put him in the Boy Scouts when he was younger and he never got into it. To him, camping was about not sleeping and getting bug bites in areas you couldn't scratch. Helen wasn't keen on it either, but she found her own ways to manage. She knew how important it was to me. She went along because she loved me. I never forgot that.

I woke up in the chair at an early hour. I knew it was early because I could see the wall clock out the corner of my eye. It was a little after seven. The birds were doing that annoying chirp they only bring out when people were trying to sleep. Normally, I would be mad, but today I was glad.

I pulled myself out of the chair and stretched hard. My body felt sore once more, but it was nothing I couldn't walk off. I filled Robert's water dish then headed for the bathroom. I stripped my clothes into a pile and stepped into the shower. I didn't even wait for the water to get hot.

The frigid water hit my unsuspecting body like cinderblocks. I reached for the faucet to move the temperature into the realm of warmth. I placed my head under the faucet for who knows how long, letting the sound of pounding water overtake my senses and making me forget that I had two days to live, maybe less.

I decided to take Robert on a long hike. As long as we were out here, we might as well appreciate the nature. I packed trail mix and bottles of water even though we probably wouldn't use them. The terrain around the cabin was still a mystery to me. Just when I thought I had the woods figured out, I would found something new that made me alter my mental map. It became a relaxing hobby of mine, just to walk in the woods and explore.

Robert and I had walked about two hours when I found some small cliffs. They were close enough together that you could jump from one to the other without much worry. Or that is what I thought. I was making the final jump when something went wrong.

Perhaps the rock was slippery. Perhaps I miscalculated the jump. I cannot be sure. One moment I was okay and next I was in the air. It was a small drop, but still enough to injure. I hit the ground face first with only newly fallen leaves as a cushion. When I hit the ground, I actually bounced before rolling once or twice. I came to a stop on my back watching the trees spin. Then it all went black.

While I was out, I dreamt of my wife. We were in an open field, with green grass as far as the eye could see. She had her back to me, her grey hair swaying in the wind. I stood next to her and waited for her to say something.

"It's beautiful isn't it?" she said finally looking at me.

"What is?" I asked.

"Everything around us, it's perfect really."

"It is," I said

Helen began to walk. I followed at her side.

"I'm disappointed in you," she said.

I sighed deeply. "I'm sorry. You at least understand why right?"

"Of course I understand. You loved me so much. When I died, it made you think that nothing could be right again."

"It hasn't been right," I snapped.

Helen forcefully grabbed my arm and locked her eyes tight to mine. She said nothing but I sure as hell got the message anyway.

"Things changed, Ryan. That didn't give you the right to give up. It is not fair to you or Daniel. You have to make it right."

"It's too late for that," I said.

Helen response to this was to laugh. She gave me her laughter. She took her hand in mine, gentler than before and squeezed.

"Ryan," she said. Helen kissed me with the soft lips my dreams were haunted by. I shut my eyes tight, but it was not meant to be. She broke the kiss.

"It's never too late," she said.

The field began to fall away as I glanced around for the escape that wasn't there. Helen wasn't afraid. She knew this would happen.

"I have to go," she said softly.

"No. Please. Helen, don't leave me," I called out. "I need you so much."

She smiled again, though it was one of sadness. Then she was gone. The field continued to disappear all around me. Then I was falling. I tried to scream, but my lungs had no air. Not a sound came out, and that's when I heard the voice.

"Are you okay?" A woman's voice asked. The darkness lifted and I was back in the forest again. My eyes focused to normalcy. She was younger than I, maybe two decades younger. She had long red hair with touches of grey, but her face was another story. It had vitality of a woman half her age. Her eyes were kind and colored in a shade of light brown I had never seen before.

"How long was I out?" I asked her, rubbing the back of my head and grimacing.

"I'm not sure," she said. "I was passing through when I heard your dog barking. Came to investigate and found you here. That was ten minutes ago. What happened?"

"I took an unplanned swan dive."

"I'd say."

It took some effort, but I pulled myself up onto my own two feet. My legs didn't have any pain so I hadn't broken anything, thankfully. My ankle was twisted slightly, but walking carefully I would be fine until I could ice it.

"My name's Tina," she said, extending her hand to shake.

I took it. "Ryan."

"So you're out here alone Ryan, just you and the dog? What's his name by the way?"

"Robert," I said, patting his head, "He's a great dog, saved my ass today. And yes, it's just us out here."

"That must be lonely. I can't imagine anyone wanting to be alone right now," Tina said.

"We manage," I replied.

"Well manage no more. You're both coming with me."

"I'm sorry?" I asked.

"I'm cooking dinner," she said, walking back towards the main trail. "You'll be my guests."

We walked until we reached a clearing that contained her cabin. I realized then that I had passed the place numerous times in my visits but never saw anyone there. Now I knew who owned it.

"Take off your shoes," Tina said at the door, "Don't want to track mud through the place."

"Yes ma'am," I said, slipping them off.

Tina's cabin was a bit more modest than mine. Little adorned the walls but she made up for it by splashing the place with random bits of color. A blanket here, a vase there, made the place feel lively.

"Beer?" she asked, opening the fridge.

"Sure," I said.

She grabbed two glass bottles and twisted the caps off in one quick motion, flicking them off to the other side of the room. She handed one to me and we clinked them together.

"Salud," she said.

"Salud," I replied.

I took a strong pull from the bottle, letting the beer slide down my throat without resistance.

"That's damn good," I said.

"It's not," Tina said. "It's a cheap ass beer, but it will do for my purposes."

"Which is?" I asked.

"Binge drink till I pass out," she said sarcastically. "With any luck, the world goes belly up and I won't be awake for it."

I laughed. "Sounds like a plan."

"I'm just messing with you. Don't actually plan to do that. I got a stack of books

I never had the chance to read. I plan to spend Sunday reading them. As many as time will allow."

"That seems like a much better plan," I said.

"I never read enough, even though I can do it quickly. I thought this might the best time to do so."

Tina motioned to the kitchen table and I took a seat. "What about you Ryan? What have you planned to do?"

"I hadn't thought that far ahead," I said truthfully.

"Sure you haven't."

"It's true. I came out here to have a few days of peace. I left it up in the air on purpose."

"Why come alone? Don't you have family?"

"I did," I said.

Tina stayed silent for a moment, realizing she hit a sore spot with me.

"I'm sorry," she said after a minute.

"It's okay," I replied

"What happened?

"I lost the wife to cancer a few years back. It broke me. I lost my relationship with my son due to that."

"Do you speak?"

"Not really," I said. "That's my fault. When Helen died I didn't want to face it, face anyone. I pushed him away."

"Why didn't you go to your son's instead of here?" Tina asked.

"I didn't think that was best," I said no longer sure if I believed myself anymore. My dream reminded me of how much I'd done wrong.

"I have a phone," Tina said, pointing down the hall. "Call him. Make it right."

I laughed. Tina looked at me as if I was mad.

"What's so funny?" she asked.

"You were the second person to tell me that today," I noted.

Tina's phone was in the bedroom. She closed the door to give me privacy. She was considerate like that. I reached for the receiver and picked it up. I dialed his number and heard it ring once, twice. When someone finally picked up it was not Daniel but the voice of a child; the voice of my granddaughter.

"Hello?" Kayla said.

"Hello there. Is your daddy home?" I asked.

"Yes. Who are you?"

"It's Grandpa, Kayla."

"Are you coming to see us?" Kayla asked, with a sweet curiosity that almost made me cry right then. I held it together somehow.

"Not right now, maybe in a few days. Let me speak to your dad."

I could hear the pitter patter of feet on the other side of the line of Kayla running to find Daniel. I was on the edge of hyperventilation. I kept trying to breathe and make it through it.

"Hi Dad," Daniel said curtly.

"Daniel." I replied.

"How's the cabin?" Daniel asked.

"It's good."

"Robert?"

"He's fine."

"Where are you calling from? I know the place doesn't have a phone," Daniel asked.

"I'm at another cabin. Not far from ours. The owner, Tina, found us and invited us to dinner."

"I see," Daniel said.

"Yeah," I replied.

A long silence permeated on the line.

"Dad, it's not too late," Daniel said.

"Too late?" I asked.

"To come home and spend time with your family, with your granddaughter. You can still make it."

"I know. I know, but I've gone too far. So many mistakes my son. I pushed you away after your mother died. I'm sorry for that. I love you. You're the best part of me. You always were."

"Don't do this Dad," Daniel said. I could hear him crying.

"It will be quite all right, don't you worry son. If we make it to Monday, I'll come by. We'll take Kayla to that park she likes, okay?"

"Sure," Daniel said. "She would like that. So would I."

The line went dead. I know he didn't hang up on me this time; the conversation wasn't going that way. Someone must have toppled a telephone line. Perhaps the whole grid had gone down. The only thing certain was that it was probably the last time I would

24

ever speak to my son. I replaced the receiver into its cradle and wept.

Tina and I sat at the couch near the fireplace sometime after, watching the fire crackle. We were nursing our seventh beers at that point and I was getting buzzed. I hadn't had that much in decades.

"Do you have kids?" I asked her.

"No," Tina replied.

"No?"

"I had some surgery in my twenties that prevented that. I regretted not having them but now—"

"Now, you won't have to have deal with the pain of them dying," I finished for her.

She nodded. "You stole the words right out of my mouth."

"I do that sometimes," I said. She politely laughed.

"I always wanted to be a mother. I know I could've adopted, but it didn't feel right. I wanted them to be my own."

"I get it," I said, nodding.

"You were blessed, Ryan. You got to marry the love of your life, and you had a great kid. It's something to be proud of."

"You're right," I said, finishing my drink, "It is."

We must've drifted off because when I came to, the fire had burned down to embers and it was pitch black outside. I looked at Tina. She was deep in sleep. I intended to keep her that way. I got up slowly, and put my jacket on. Robert was awake and laying on the floor next to the door. I motioned for him to get up and quietly opened the door. He darted out into the clearing as I took one last look.

She was still safe in dreams. I prayed they were pleasant. She kept me from going to the brink. There were no words for that kind of gratitude. Her head tilted to the left but she didn't stir.

I closed the door. It was time to go.

It took some time in the dark but we found the way back. I started a fire and gave Robert some more dog food. He had eaten plenty but I didn't care. He dug in with relish. As for me, I chomped on saltine crackers and consumed cups of water to counter my intoxication. I sure as hell didn't want a hangover for my last morning on earth.

The recliner looked cozy once again so I plopped myself into it. Robert finished eating and jumped on top of my lap, wanting to be petted. We sat together and felt seconds tick away.

"It's just you and me boy," I said, rubbing my hands across his fur, "Just you and me."

I had another dream. It was the three of us at the cabin. Daniel was four and full of energy. He wasn't jaded about nature then. He reveled in it. Many times he'd come back with his clothes caked in dirt and grime. It drove his mother mad. I think he did it on purpose sometimes, just to mess with her. I didn't mind that. I was glad he was seeing what I did.

Helen would just shake her head at the two boys God had placed her with and tried to finish the latest Danielle Steele novel while we were off being men. She didn't understand it, but she appreciated it on some level. It gave her some much desired quiet time, which was always in short supply.

The last night we were there, Daniel had fallen asleep early so we tucked him into bed. I wanted to take a night walk. Helen, who hated them most of the time, surprisingly agreed to my request. We walked for a few minutes and found a clearing where the sky was not blocked by foliage. The sky was in full bloom, the stars dotting the world with bright lights.

"They're beautiful aren't they?" she asked.

"What is?"

"The stars," she said.

And then I woke up. I checked the time. It was nine a.m. If anything was going to happen, I didn't know how. I didn't know when. I didn't know why. All I knew is I was going to face it. However, it would not be on an empty stomach.

I moved into the kitchen where I made the ultimate breakfast. I thought nothing of wasting food. Pancakes, eggs, bacon, toast. I made it all and I intended to eat it all. I placed plate after plate on the table and began to dig in. Robert wagged his tail at the foot of the table and I threw samples at his feet, which he happily devoured.

I ate quickly, feeling like a stuffed pig afterwards. Normally I would've passed out in

27

a food coma, but I wasn't done. I took a long shower, scrubbing my body till it felt raw. I changed into fresh clothes and laced up my hiking boots tight. With Robert at my side, I walked into the forest that always seemed endless to me.

There were many paths to travel.

I intended to find them.

JASON

The gun felt cool, heavy in my hand. I was nervous, my palms greased with sweat. I almost dropped the damn thing. I jerked the slide back, chambering the first and only round I'd need. I flicked the safety off with a swipe of my thumb. It was ready. I was ready.

I wrote my suicide note. I thought about it a lot. I thought of my parents whom I loved despite their cluelessness and Martin who was my only friend. This wasn't their fault. They couldn't have stopped it. I didn't want to hurt anymore. Writing the letter took time. I wanted it perfect.

I folded the piece of paper in two, creasing the middle. I wrote my name on the blank side in all caps. It could not be missed. I placed the barrel in my mouth, tasting the gun oil. I shut my eyes tight. Five pounds of pressure, I thought. Five pounds was standing between me and peace.

That moment never came. Seconds ticked away and the gun was still in my mouth. I removed it and placed it back down. I banged my fists on the table, making it jump. My scream was primal, as loud as my lungs would allow.

I am a fucking coward.

I was never a lucky one. To live a life bereft of complication. To have everything I wanted. That was not in the cards. I was dealt a life not worth living. I spent nights wondering why. Every day felt worse than the last. Nothing changed, nothing got better.

There is part of me deep down. It continues to spread and it's getting harder to keep at bay. Why haven't I given up? I think it's because I still cling to a sliver of hope. That everything will be okay. Then on Thursday the world decided it wanted to end. It just proved my theory of life being shit.

I was hanging out with Martin. Martin was my best friend, the only one I had. It was a necessity for both of us. No one would have guys like us for friends. That night, we were partaking in some greasy take out from some hole in the wall burger joint. After our hearty meals were consumed, we sat down to watch a flick. I had chosen something different. It was an assassin flick with George Clooney. In it, he's a methodical killer whose undoing is love.

The movie ended and the credits began to roll. Martin looked at me and shook his head. He seemed displeased.

"You didn't like it?" I asked.

"No," he said, throwing his hands in the air in exasperation. "Not at all."

"Why?"

"It was boring. Nothing happened. It was George Clooney walking around a village for ninety minutes."

"It was much more than that," I retorted.

"No it wasn't. The chick was hot though. I'll give it that."

"That's the only thing you notice; explosions and tits."

"That's why Michael Bay is a marketing genius. He gives the people what they want."

"But the people are stupid," I shot back.

"That doesn't matter if it sells. Sorry, but the movie blew."

"Well, I thought it was a good movie," I said.

"You would. You're obsessed with that art house shit," Martin said.

He switched the TV back over to cable. I sighed, shaking my head and went to the kitchen for a beer. I was going to need it.

We almost didn't realize something was happening. One minute we're waiting for a commercial break to end and the next we were staring at a white screen.

"What the hell?" Martin said.

"It's one of those emergency broadcast tests," I said.

"There would be a screeching beeping noise by now. This is something else."

He was right. Letters begin to dance across the screen, until a simple short message was typed. It was so on point, it was almost laughable. We didn't laugh, we didn't do anything. We stared at the screen as if our life depended on it. The message went away and the feed went back to normal. Our show was back on, but we didn't care. We looked at each other.

"What is going on man?" Martin said, scared.

"It's nothing dude," I said, trying to be reassuring. "It's got to be a joke or something."

Nope. Every channel was taken over by news coverage. All those channels cut to live coverage of the President. He told us not to panic. There was nothing to fear. We should just stay in our homes and everything was under control.

What a crock of shit, I thought. This was just what I needed; yet another reason to hate my life. It was bad enough that I was depressed, now the whole damn world was going to hell. It was just fucking perfect. Martin, well, he was white as a sheet; he clearly believed it.

"What are we going to do, Jason?" he asked me, his voice cracking.

"Calm down, Martin. None of this means anything," I said.

"Calm down? Jesus, they got the President of the United States telling us not to panic! They take this seriously man. This isn't some crackpot religious nut. This is real."

"Maybe you're right, maybe not," I said, holding my cards close to the chest.

"I don't understand how you can be so calm," he said.

"I'm just trying to see all the angles," I replied. I stood up and headed for the door.

"Where are you going man?" Martin asked.

"I'm going home. I'll come by tomorrow," I said.

When I got home, my answering machine was blinking furiously. I had messages; who knew, somebody loved me. I pressed the button. I had six messages total. Not shabby. As they began to play, my good mood vanished. They were all from Mom and Dad. Five were from Mom and just one from dear old Dad. Shows disparity of parental love doesn't it?

I guess I should explain a little bit in regards to my family. When I was seven, my parents went through the definition of a nasty divorce. Lamps were thrown; court orders were delivered, the whole nine yards. Neither of them looked like a saint, and as precedents usually go, I was placed with my mother. My father was granted weekend custody. At first, I was cool with it. Then as time passed it became more difficult to deal with her.

My mom has a lot of regret. Not about me, that would be fucked up. No, she had regrets about other things. She didn't go to college for it was a different time than now. She went straight into the workforce right out of high school and worked at the same place all her life. She didn't go anywhere or do anything in a sense. She resented that things were beyond her control. My heart broke for her, for she never felt she was good enough. I tried to tell her otherwise, but she never believed me. If you can't believe in yourself, you're sunk. I knew that better than anyone.

My father was different. He was tough, but fair. He loved me. I was his boy; nothing could change that, even divorce. But it's difficult to forge a relationship on two days a week. As I got older, we drifted apart. It was an inevitable that we wouldn't see eye to eye. We didn't know how to talk to each other.

There was none of the deep, personal conversations you should have with your child. He didn't know how to connect with me. When something personal came up I went to somebody else. When I tried to tell him things, he usually berated me for not knowing the right answer already. I was getting to the age where I was trying to figure out what I wanted in life. I couldn't figure it out and was afraid to tell him that. It led him to believe I was aimless, slacker. Maybe I was.

In spite of all our problems, I was going to pick up the phone and call them because family is family. They would speak quietly about the news and what it meant. Ever the dutiful son, I would assuage their fears and tell them nothing bad was going to happen.

Well, at least not yet.

I called Dad first, since I knew I would be on the phone all night with Mom. One great thing about talking with your father is that the conversations are direct and to the point; as they should be. After a few rings, he finally picked up. His voice was flat, but with a touch of concern.

"Jason?" he said.

"Yeah," I said.

"Thank God. Where were you when I called?"

"I was at Martin's," I said.

"So you know?" he asked.

I sighed. "Yeah, we saw."

"Are you okay?" he finally asked.

"What do you mean?" I said.

"With everything they're saying. It's heavy stuff."

"I've accepted it."

"That's mighty quick of you," he said. He obviously didn't believe me.

"I'll deal in my own way," I said. "I'm fine."

"I'm not," he said. "I lived a good life, but there's a lot of things you won't have opportunities for, that bothers me. You're my son; I want you to be happy."

"Dad," I said, trying my very best to sound convincing. "Monday is going to roll around and we'll have a big laugh about this over a couple beers. Okay?"

My father chuckled. He did that when he was nervous.

"Sure. I want you to see you though, just in case."

"I'll call you," I said.

"That's fine."

"Dad," I said.

"Yeah," he said.

I paused for a moment.

"You know that I love you right?" I asked.

"I know son. Me too," he replied.

I won't bore you with the minute details involving my call to Mom. You've learned a little about her so I think you can fill in the gaps. For those wanting the cliff notes I shall indulge thee. It lasted almost two hours. I know because I timed it. Mom cried a lot. She said everything was going to end in a baptism of fire. Her words, not mine. She called me her "Baby Boy" on several occasions and normally I would have been annoyed by it, but considering the circumstances I let it slide. I did my best to console her, but her mind was set in stone. She wanted to see me and I told her I would come by the next day.

I went into the kitchen and poured myself the tallest rum my glass would allow. I downed the bitch in two gulps, it seemed appropriate. The walls of vice would crumble in the face of Armageddon. Sober people would drink. Addicts would snort. Virgins would fuck. You might want do it all before it was too late. I had done enough. The only precipice I hadn't crossed was my own death. That was being handled for me. It was out of my control. The universe was fucking me again, and I hated that.

Fuck that. This was my life. I intended to go out on my terms. A cool, calming wave crashed over me. In that moment, I finally had control.

Just on the outskirts of town there is an old bridge that overlooks the river. The river is rather dangerous; raging vortexes of water that smashed upon jagged rocks. You had to be crazy to go swimming in that water. Some had been, and their bodies weren't usually found. It would be the perfect place.

On Sunday morning I would step onto the edge and let myself fall. Fly towards peace. It was simple, poetic even. I glanced towards the kitchen counter where the clock stood. It was no longer a clock. It had become a glorious drummer, marching me forward to my final resting place. It was divine, this ticking clock.

I woke up refreshed Friday morning. I didn't feel the water hit my skin as I showered. I had other things on my mind. I ate breakfast and quickly dressed. There was much to do.

I was going to see Martin first. Martin had lived alone ever since his father died and his mom ran off with a trucker few years back. Luckily for him, the house was already paid off. He had offered me to live there as a roommate, but I politely declined. I liked having my own space.

The first thing I noticed when I got there was a maroon sedan parked on the sidewalk next to his house that I didn't recognize. It was probably just a neighbor's car, or maybe Martin had some female company. You never knew with him.

I rapped my fist against the door. No one answered. I rapped harder. Finally, after what seemed like forever, he finally came to the door. His curly black hair was all over the place. His skin was pale, almost translucent, and Martin needed sun badly.

"Jason?" Martin said over a yawn. "You do realize it is morning right?"

"I know that," I said, anxious. "I told you I'd come over. Now pull yourself together and let's do something."

"Do what?" he asked.

"I don't know man, something fun. We only have so long, so get dressed and let's go."

"I can't," he said, his eyes arching down.

"Why?" I asked.

"I have company," he replied.

"I knew it!" I said, a little louder than I intended. "You got some action last night! Good for you. Hope she didn't crush you."

"No, Jason, my mom came home," Martin said.

My jaw dropped.

"When did she come back?" I asked.

"Last night right after you left. She wanted to be home with me," Martin said.

"That doesn't excuse the last three years."

"She's trying man, and I'm glad she's here."

I grinned. "That's good man. Now let's go, she can wait a bit."

"I don't think that's such a good idea," Martin said, his voice flat.

"What are you talking about?" I asked.

"You think I don't know?"

"Know what? Spit it out."

"I found your note," Martin said grimly.

I suddenly felt lightheaded. I had tossed the note in a drawer under some papers. He must've found it looking for a pen or something. So, the cat was out of the bag.

"And?" I asked nonchalantly, as if it was no big deal.

"I can't be part of it," Martin said. He sighed deep. "I know I should be making every effort to make sure you don't do it, but I read that note. Nothing I say will matter to you. I need to spend some time with my mom.

Reconnect before time runs out. I'm sorry, forgive me man."

Then, just like that, he shut the door in my face. My best friend had just bailed on me. I considered breaking the door down with my fists. Scream until my lungs gave out. I did none of these things. It would just be wasted energy.

It was becoming difficult to drive in town. The place was a wreck. Broken shop windows, overturned cars, debris in the streets; every apocalyptic cliché you could think of. The silver lining of the chaos was it kept my mind on making sure I didn't crash. In doing that I could forget my only friend abandoned me. If there was anyone that could've talked me out of it, it was him. He only wound up strengthening my resolve. If he wouldn't help me, what was the point in living?

I was so wrapped up in my thoughts I almost didn't see her. There was a woman my age being chased down the street by two guys, and they seemed to mean business. Every fiber in my being told me to ignore it; it wasn't my problem, but something made me apply pressure to the brake, stopping the car in the middle of the road. I turned off the engine and went after them.

I followed the three down a narrow alleyway. I kept my distance and hid behind a dumpster. I wanted to be absolutely sure I wasn't walking into a misunderstanding.

"Where you going baby?" The first guy asked, "We're not gonna hurt you."

"Yeah, we just wanna have some fun," the second one said.

This was not a drill. I knew what "fun" meant.

"Stay away from me," the girl said.

"Or what?" the first guy said.

I could see it in the look on her face that she didn't have a good answer.

They laughed and had every right to. The ball was in their court, or so they thought. I glanced down and saw a piece of pipe that would be most helpful. I tested its weight. It would do.

"We're not going to ask again," the first guy said.

"Fuck you," the girl sneered, spitting in his direction.

"I plan to—"

"I don't think so," I said, coming out into the open, pipe in hand. Their faces primarily showed surprise then bravado. Then they saw the pipe, and their expressions changed.

"Who the fuck are you?" The first guy asked.

"I'm her boyfriend," I mockingly replied, giving her a wave. "Hi honey."

Her expression was priceless.

"Get lost. This doesn't concern you," the second one said.

"Does now," I said.

"Why you care?" the first one asked.

"I don't know," I said with a glimmer of truth. "But I'm here."

We were at a standstill. I was on one side and the girl on the other. Two thugs stood between us and they had no proclivities about harming either of us. I was outnumbered, but I held one hell of an advantage in my hand.

"You should just leave now," I said firmly.

"Is that so?" the first one asked.

"Yes," I said.

"Fuck this. Let's kick his ass," the second one said.

"Your move," I replied.

I don't like confrontation. I've only been in a handful of fights and most of them ended with me getting my ass handed to me. However, when you have a pipe in your hand, you don't have to be a martial arts champion. It does most of the work for you.

Mr. Bravado went down first. He charged me and easily walked into my swing that thudded into his gut. He doubled over in pain and squeaked out a groan. A follow up strike to his left arm shattered bone. It hung limp like a ragdoll.

"You broke my arm, you fuck!" he screamed.

"It appears I did," I quipped.

One more hit to the back of his head and he was out cold. His buddy was a different story. He wasn't an idiot, unlike his friend. I swung the pipe, but he quickly deflected it, and it slipped out of my hand, clanging down the alleyway. If he had followed that up with some quick punches I would've probably folded up. As it turned out, he wasn't as smart as I thought. He chose to gloat instead, thinking now that the outlook had already been decided.

"What are you going to do now?" he sneered.

I used his momentary inattention to hit him with a full body tackle. I slammed him into the ground, knocking the air out of him. He was down, but not out, as he hit me with a left jab. I ignored the pain that burned through my body and focused on hurting him. I kept hitting him until I saw blood. Content, I stood up and searched the ground for the pipe. I recovered it and checked on the girl.

The girl had stayed in the same spot the whole time. I wondered if she was more afraid of me than them. I waved my hand across her face to get her out of the trance she was in, and she snapped to attention.

"You okay?" I asked.

She nodded.

"What's your name?" I asked.

"Jenna," she said.

"I'm Jason. Just stay back for the moment," I said.

The first guy began coughing and tried to get up. I quickly ended that endeavor with a swift kick to the chest. He stayed down that time. I couched and met him at his level.

"Didn't go the way you planned, did it?" I asked.

He gave no response outside mumbled swearing.

"Of course it didn't. You didn't expect some guy to ruin your 'party'," I said, looking back at Jenna. She hung to my every word.

"I hate people like you," I said, my voice going cold. "I told myself long ago, if anyone EVER harmed a woman like that, I'd put him in the ground. No arrests, no courts, no nothing. He'd go six feet under. I'll cut you some slack and not make any rash judgments today."

I pointed to Jenna. He looked at her.

"And believe me, I want to, but she doesn't. I can tell. Even with what you planned to do to her, she doesn't wish you harm. So I won't do it. You both get to leave alive," I said.

Through wincing, the first guy breathed relief.

"However," I said. "That doesn't mean I'm done with you."

"What?" the first guy said in disbelief.

My hand holding the pipe quickly shot out and struck down hard on his genitals. He yelped.

"That hurt?" I asked. "I imagine it does."

I kicked him once more for good measure.

Surprisingly to me, my car hadn't been stolen or destroyed in the time I was gone. I gingerly placed the now catatonic Jenna in the passenger seat while I returned to the driver's side, and I got us the hell out of there. I had to put distance between us and that alley. Jenna said nothing. I tried to read her expressions, but her blonde hair kept getting in the way. I decided to keep my eyes on the road.

I knew nothing about this girl, and the roads were getting worse.

"Jenna," I said. "Do you want me to take you home?"

"I don't care where we go right now," she said.

"I need to think. How about I take you to my apartment, and afterwards I'll drive you anywhere you want to go."

"Okay," she said.

My apartment was a mess. Like a nervous boy bringing a girl home for the first time, I hastily cleaned up while Jenna sat in the kitchen.

"I never have guests over," I explained.

I sounded foolish, though she didn't seem to notice. She nodded, taking my statement at face value. I made coffee and placed a cup next to her.

"Jenna," I said.

Without realizing it, I had placed my hand on top of hers. She noticed, but she didn't pull away.

"Why were you out there?" I asked.

"Excuse me?"

"I mean, in case you haven't noticed, the world is going down the tubes. It's not safe to be alone out there."

She shook her head. "I was trying to see a friend, but she was gone. Then those guys came after me and they would've got me if you hadn't shown up."

"It was nothing," I said nonchalantly.

"It was brave, thank you," she said.

"Don't mention it," I replied. "Can we talk about something else? I really don't want to think about it anymore."

"Sure," she said, "What would you rather discuss?"

"Anything," I said, "Ask me anything."

Jenna told me a bit about her childhood. I told her about mine. We pinged from one topic to the next until we inevitably returned to the true elephant in the room; our impending doom and people's reaction to it.

"It's unreal how people have been acting," she said.

"I agree," I said.

"Everything is mad out there, and we cannot be even sure that any of it is true. It's becoming self-fulfilling," she said.

"Yeah," I replied.

"Can I ask you something?" she asked.

"Sure," I said.

"What did you plan to do on Sunday? You know, before everything happens."

What she wanted to know, I never intended to share with anyone. This was something you definitely didn't bring up in casual conversation.

"I rather not talk about it," I said, guarded.

"Okay," she replied her tone anything but. Silence filled the room once more.

"Do you want me to take you home?" I asked, changing the subject.

"Trying to get rid of me?" she asked.

"Not at all," I said, "but I have a dinner to attend."

"With whom?" she asked.

"My mom," I said.

"Can I tag along?" she asked.

"You want to?"

"Sure," she said, "I'd rather not be alone right now anyway."

My mother doesn't live far from my apartment, but the roads got worse if that was even possible. I was dodging debris left and right the whole way there.

"What should I tell her?" I asked Jenna.

"Tell her about what?"

"About how we met," I said.

"That's easy. Say we met at a bookstore," she said.

"A bookstore?" I asked puzzled.

"Good as any cover story. It makes our meeting sound legitimate. The guy gets to look like he has decent social skills and I get to not look like a tramp."

Jenna flashed a smile. "Which of course," she joked. "I am not."

We arrived a little after six. The neighborhood looked untouched by the carnage a few miles away. I guess people from the suburbs still had a sense of balance, even during the end of the world. A person's home was off limits. The streets were fair game.

I mentally prepared myself for what Mom might do. I never introduced a girl to either of my parent's before. My timing just made it that much worse. By the end of the night, she would be crying that she will never see grandchildren. That wasn't my fault of course, but I would still be the asshole in the equation. You can't win against that kind of twisted logic.

Mom looked very happy to see me. She had been stunning in her youth and was still a lovely woman in her later years. She had deep blue eyes, a demure smile that made you think she was always up to something, and a figure that turned heads even now. Dad was a moron for ever letting her go.

"Jason," Mom said. "I'm so glad you came." She then saw Jenna and her surprise was palpable. "And you brought a friend?"

"Yeah," I said. "Mom, this is Jenna. Jenna, this is my mother, Erica.

"Nice to meet you, dear," Mom said.

"Nice to meet you," Jenna replied.

"Come on in, you two, before you catch cold," Mom said, ushering us inside.

Mom made my favorite casserole. As I ate, Jenna and Mom talked. Mom asked all the important questions and Jenna answered like a pro. Mom remained in the dark as to how we really met. I spoke up once in a while, but I knew to stay out of it overall. It wasn't my conversation. I left them to it.

I cleaned the table afterwards and washed the dishes. It was simple logic. Mom had cooked, so the least I could do was clean and it gave them more time to talk. I finished up and dried my hands with a kitchen towel. Mom pulled me aside.

"I like her," Mom said, "I'm glad you brought her along."

"I'm glad you got along so good," I said.

"I just wish," Mom said, her voice choking up. "That you had met her sooner."

I hugged her. She had no idea how her words were on point.

"I know Mom, me too," I said.

I drove Jenna home afterwards. She lived on the other side of town, but the roads I had to use were free of hindrances so we moved at a fast clip. I parked the car outside her apartment, the radio playing the acoustic version of "Plush" by Stone Temple Pilots.

"I like this song," I said.

"Me too," she replied.

"Can I see you tomorrow?"

"Okay," she said, "Seven p.m.?"

"Fine by me."

"Okay then," she said, before jumping out the car. "See you later."

My favorite thing to do is to play the guitar. It's the only thing that makes me remotely happy. Most people don't know I play. If I had mentioned it to others, perhaps it would have opened more doors for me socially, but most had already made up their minds. To them, I wasn't worth knowing, so screw them.

I wasn't a novice who paid a hack to teach them a few chords. I was self taught and by working at my own pace it allowed to learn on my own terms. Martin was the only one I shared this with and he was particularly awestruck by my progress.

Soon, I began writing my own songs. I never intended to do anything with them. I sing off key so a solo endeavor was out. When it came to me joining a band, remember I have a problem with other people. The problem being that most people are assholes. The idea of sharing my work with those who would not appreciate it made my stomach turn.

I hooked my amp up when I got back home. I placed the volume loud, but not deafening. In the past, I had been given two citations for noise violations, but that was no longer a threat. The police were off making sure society didn't collapse before its regularly scheduled time. So my neighbors could bite me.

As my thoughts had regularly drifted towards suicide, the idea of writing a final song intrigued me. All the great artists do it. Mozart before he died young and penniless was in the middle of writing his magnum opus "The Requiem Mass." It seemed like a good thing to do. An artist's final say before they shuffle off the mortal coil. I would find my own, and let it be my unknown gift to the world.

The sun beamed directly into my eyes and woke me prematurely. The sun and I had never been friends. I gave it the finger and cursed. I was tired, but I knew I couldn't sleep in. I left my warm bed reluctantly, and the bathroom never felt so far away.

I stared into the mirror and knew I had seen better days. My hair jutted out in twelve different directions and was in dire need of a trim. The stubble on my face was getting out of control. My eyes were bloodshot and had dark rings that circled them, but I was willing to bet everybody had them. In the end, it was nothing a shower couldn't fix so that became my first priority. I used cold water instead of hot. I was an ice cube, but clean and most importantly alert. I furiously dried myself, feeling ready to face the day.

I called my father first thing, and he sounded no different than the night before. We were going to meet at his house. Dad's house was in the opposite direction of Mom's. It was if they needed to also live as far apart as possible. After a quick bite, I was out the door.

The first thing I notice was how quiet the streets were, with not a soul in sight. I guess everyone got tired of rioting. If that meant I wouldn't cross paths with any psychos that was okay in my book. I was struck by the irony and laughed. I'd been trying to kill myself and yet I was afraid someone was going to kill me. I chalked it up to not wanting to checkout before I said when.

Dad's neighborhood was untouched as well. What really got me was that people were outside doing things. Kids were playing in the backyard while their mother's watched behind the pages of trashy romance novels. The husband's were in the garages fixing things or mowing the lawn. It was surreal imagery, as if the announcement fell on deaf ears.

I didn't even have to knock. Dad swung open the door at my arrival. He walked up to me and gave me a hug. It was strange; he had never been overly affectionate.

"Glad you could make it," Dad said.

"No problem," I replied.

"Come on in," he said.

The house was dark. Dad never liked too many lights. He was one of those guys that worried about the bill every month. It took a moment for my eyes to adjust, but I found my way around.

"Can I get you anything, coffee, water?" he asked.

"No. I'm good," I said.

"I'm going to get a bottle of water. Be right back."

Dad left to go into the kitchen. I sat on the couch and waited. With nothing better to do, I studied the family photos. My dad had plenty of them out. Some were black and white with him and his brother Dave. Another had Mom and him in happier times. The rest were of me. One in particular stood out. It was Dad and me at a circus. I was about three and riding on his shoulders. I remember that day being perfect. I spent the day watching people ride elephants and do flips. I got to spend time with my hero, my Dad.

We all wish it could stay like that, when things were simpler. It's when we're older that we realize things aren't perfect. Your heroes have flaws, just like everyone else. They do bad things too, even to those they love most.

"Sorry I took so long," Dad said, returning to the living room.

"No big deal," I said.

"Looking at photos?"

"Yeah," I said, pointing at the two of us. "That's my favorite."

"Mine too," he said, sitting down. "So, your mother tells me you met someone."

I winced. We never really talked about girls.

"Yeah, her name is Jenna," I said.

"You like her?" he asked.

"We just met."

"You can't use that excuse, not now. You want some unsolicited advice from your old man?"

I sighed. "You're going to tell me no matter my response."

"Damn right I will," he said. "Spend your time with her and be grateful for it. Your folks fucked up the best thing we ever had. Now we have no one, so we're having to face this alone."

"You're not alone," I said.

Dad smiled.

"Thanks son," he said, capping his water bottle. "How about we shoot some hoops?

"Sure Dad," I said. "I'd like that."

We shot hoops for the rest of the afternoon. Dad won most of the games. His knees were bad so he couldn't move like he used to, but he could dribble and dodge in ways I'll never be able to. What I lacked in short game, however, I made up by being tall. I put him in his place with a humiliating block or two. It was just the type of bonding we needed to do. We never did it enough, but one only notices that in hindsight.

When we had finished playing for the day, we sat on the porch and sipped cold lemonade. We didn't talk much. We were content to watch the world go by. It was after four by then and the kids were almost tired from playing. They would eat dinner and then rebound for more mischief before bed. Even being a former child, I didn't know how they did it.

"What's on the agenda tonight?" Dad asked.

"Go home and shower. Play guitar. Go see Jenna. Not sure beyond that," I said.

"Not bad."

"What about you?" I asked him.

"I think I'll watch the sun set," he said somberly. "It might be the last one I'll ever see."

I jumped in the shower the second I got home and changed into some new clothes. I grabbed my guitar and headed for Jenna's. She said come on over and besides I wanted to take Dad's advice to heart.

I knocked on her door and waited. I knew she lived on the first floor because I watched her enter the previous night. When she opened the door, she looked happy to see me.

"Howdy stranger," she said. "What brings you here?"

"I thought I'd cook you dinner," I said.

Her eyebrows arched. "You cook?"

"Yes ma'am," I said.

"It's like I don't know you at all," she said, jokingly, waving me inside.

I cooked pasta. I don't actually cook, but even I couldn't screw that up. Jenna seemed to think it was perfection, using every other bite telling me how good it was.

"That hit the spot," she said as we finished up.

"My pleasure," I said.

"Thank you."

"Really, it's no big deal—"

"No, Jason," she said. "Thank you. You saved my life."

I didn't know how to respond. I was no hero. I had no illusions on who I was.

"We never talked about it," she said.

"No," I said. "We didn't. I'll say one thing though."

"Yeah?" she asked.

"I don't regret helping you," I said.

"Well, I'm glad you did," she said.

"I brought you something else," I said, hastily changing the subject.

"Other than delicious food?" she inquired. "Tell me, I can't stand the suspense."

"I brought my guitar," I said. "I thought I'd play for you."

"You're a musician?" she asked.

"Self taught," I added.

"Cool," she replied.

I set my amp up in her living room and plugged the guitar into the jack. I decided to keep the volume somewhat low so I didn't knock her back into a wall or something. I played a few notes and adjusted the strings accordingly.

"What are you going to play for me?" Jenna asked, sitting at the foot of the bed.

"Not sure," I said, "Got any requests?"

"Surprise me," she said.

I began to play a few notes. A few notes turned into something more. I had no idea where it was all coming from, but it flowed together beautifully. It was as if I took all my pain, my sorrow, and strummed it all out right then and there. When it was over, I felt chilled. Jenna was breathing hard, and I think she was crying.

"What was that called?" she asked.

I turned off the amp and placed my guitar on the floor.

"Requiem," I said.

We were lying in bed. We held each other, fully clothed, making no overtures to fool around. Hell, we hadn't even kissed. We were just two lost souls looking for companionship. I was okay with that. It was what I needed. I could now be honest with her.

"I was going to kill myself," I confessed.

That definitely got her attention.

"Excuse me?" she asked.

"You asked me before what my plan was for tomorrow. I was going to off myself. Jump off the bridge at the edge of town."

"Why?" she asked, genuinely shocked.

"I'd been depressed for a quite a while," I explained. "When this happened, it was the final straw. I didn't want to be here when it all went down."

"But if it didn't happen—"she began.

I shrugged. "I'd still have peace."

"God, I'm so sorry," she said.

"It's okay. It's not your fault," I said. I debated telling her more; might as well. "I tried to kill myself two weeks ago."

"What happened?" she asked.

"The gun was in my mouth, and I couldn't pull the trigger," I said. "And now I know why. I was supposed to save you from harm. Things aren't so bad; I feel something I haven't felt in a long time."

"What?" she asked, holding me closer.

"I don't feel like jumping anymore," I said.

I woke up Sunday morning expecting to see Jenna sleeping by my side. She wasn't. I called out for her and searched her apartment. I didn't find her, but I did notice that her keys and phone were missing. I then found the note. It contained a single sentence. "Meet me at the bridge."

When I got to the bridge, Jenna was perched on the other side of the rail, holding on tight. I walked up slowly so I wouldn't startle her. She had already seen me though.

"How about you come back over to solid ground?" I asked.

"Afraid I'll jump?" she asked coyly.

"Afraid you'll slip," I clarified.

"Okay," she said, giving me her hand and I pulled her over the railing.

"What were you doing?" I asked her.

"Waiting for you," she said. "Plus, I was working up some adrenaline. Feel my heart."

She placed my hand on her chest. She was right. It was beating like mad.

"Let's take a breather," I said. I took a seat down on the ground and she joined me.

"Why'd you come here?" I asked. "Are you mocking me?"

"No," she said. "Absolutely not, it was just a symbolic gesture."

"Symbolic?"

"Yes. You were going to end your life here. So what better place to spend our final hours," she said. "Perhaps it will be the starting point, for a new beginning."

"Did you at least bring snacks?" I asked half jokingly. "We might be here for awhile."

"Got a cooler," she said, pointing to the left of us.

"Good," I said. "You have to be prepared."

"Always," she replied.

We sat at the edge of the bridge, watching the raging river flow. I wasn't sure how long we would have, but at least I wouldn't be dying alone. My mind, once dark and cloudy was no longer so. I had but one thought that was clear. That thought was as bright as the sun that was shining down on both our heads.

I wanted to live.

AARON

There are misconceptions about writers. It is one thing to read a book, to write one is something entirely different. Anyone can write, but it takes a person of true determination to see it through to the end. The world is full of wannabe's, of would, could, should. A true writer doesn't think "what if". He doesn't give a shit about what the world thinks of him. When he writes, he is free.

That leads into another myth. People believe that success for a writer is simple to attain. The world is full of published literature. If other authors can do it, it shouldn't be difficult for me. Wrong; no one prepares you for the difficulties you will face. Being a novelist is one of the most painstaking career paths you can choose. If you want less stress in life go work in finance, or take up medicine. Being a writer is like being bi-polar; your days are filled with soaring highs and crashing lows. The lows come with much more frequency.

The question remains, why anyone would choose this. Why would I want this? The answer to that question for me was that I wanted to leave a mark on the world. Something that said, "I was here. I mattered." It comes across as petty when you say it aloud. However, everyone wants acceptance, and I didn't have much in my life. My writing was a surrogacy of sorts; my means to fill the missing gaps. That's what I thought at least.

I'm just a guy with a dream. In that regard, I guess I'm no different than no one else.

My problem was I had yet to finish a novel. That needs clarification. I do write and write often. However, I have the strangest, rather annoying form of writer's block. I don't know how to end my work. I'll start a new project and get really deep into it. Then when it's time to do the final stretch, I clam up. All my ideas, my motivations just disappear. I spend days sitting at a blank screen, trying to figure it out, but to no avail. After a week of this inaction, I start to believe the story was shit from the beginning and then scrap the whole thing, thinking that next time, I will get it right.

The "getting it right" part has yet to occur. I've tried everything to make this affliction stop. Nothing has worked, but I haven't given up. I press on, and continue to write. My drive to join the elite club of published authors is what keeps me going. If I lost that drive, if I gave up my dream, I'd have nothing. At that point, I might as well be dead.

My writer's block has caused me to tread water in my daily life. Eventually, people get tired of it. My girlfriend Rebecca especially was exhausted. She decided to break up with me.

"I can't do this anymore," she said.

We were at Red Bowl, a Chinese restaurant two blocks from my place. We went there because I said they had good food. That was a lie. We both knew it. We went there because it was the only place I could afford. Our entire relationship had revolved around cheap Asian cuisine.

"What are you talking about?" I asked even though I knew what she meant. This was a long time coming. I give her props for staying with me this long. She must've really loved me. Not anymore.

"This," she said.

"Oh," I replied, all I could muster.

"It's not that I don't love you. I do. We're not moving forward though because you're stuck. You've been trying to do this novel for so long you have never stopped to think that maybe you're not cut out for it."

"I've just had some bad luck. Things are going to change," I said.

She wore a strange smile. The type girls wear when they know something cannot be fixed.

"No they won't," she said simply.

I sat there, chopsticks in hand knowing there was nothing I could say. I accepted it. Some battles you just can't win.

"I'm sorry Becks. You know that right?" I said.

She nodded. "I'm going to go. Okay?"

"Okay."

She put on her tan coat and slung her purse over her shoulder.

"Goodbye, Aaron," she said.

"Goodbye, Rebecca," I replied.

She began to walk away before quickly pivoting back and returning to the table.

"Aaron?" she said.

"Yes," I said.

"Do one thing for me."

"Anything, Becks."

"Prove me wrong," she said.

I went home with the very intention of doing that. I did all my pre-writing preparations. I shut away all distractions. I turned off my cell phone. I brewed a strong pot of coffee. Everything was in place. Now all I needed was an idea, any idea.

If I may impart another piece of wisdom from the writing trenches, it's this; great ideas are hard to come by. Everyone has ideas. The key to a stellar one is sustainability. A story idea has to be interesting to the writer. It must be simple to execute, but complex enough so one can stretch it out thousands of words. You have to stay on point when you write. If you don't know how to execute the idea, you're sunk before you even have a chance to finish.

However, this tidbit is overshadowed by the most important rule of being a writer. That is to write. It is okay to brainstorm, but one must not wait for the muse to grace them with inspiration. The muse will strike in the creation, not before. Your main concern is to procure the first draft no matter how bad it is, and believe me it will be bad.

Hemingway said it best. "The first draft of anything is shit." But it will be yours, and no one can ever take that from you. The editing will be even a greater test of character. There will be long nights and empty coffee cups, but if you press through the discomfort you will find yourself with a completed work. That has eluded me for years.

Well, no more, I was going to bang out a bestseller starting tonight. I would show everyone. I'll have the publishers eating out of my hand. My parents will see all my sacrifices were worth it. Rebecca will take me back.

I powered up the laptop and clicked on Microsoft Word. The cursor blinked at me ready to be moved. I placed my fingertips to the keys.

And nothing happened.

The Fucking Wall.

It's a writer's worst nightmare; the infuriating inability to get a single word down. It decided to rear its ugly head against me once more. I didn't want to see it, yet there it was. The cursor blinked, mocking me. I pulled my eyes away from the screen, attempting to jot some ideas on a yellow pad. Nothing came to mind. I was staring down another blank page. I was getting nowhere, which was becoming the story of my life.

When writers have a bad night, they deal with stress in different ways. Some exercise, some watch a favorite movie. I drink, but only on rare occasions. When things get bad like tonight, I have a bottle of Grey Goose I keep in the freezer. I pulled it out and filled a glass close to the rim. I stared at the dancing ice cubes and took a long draw. The burn felt good to my frazzled nerves. I poured another. Soon enough, I was drunk just like my first night at college.

I stumbled to my bed and by the Grace of God, found it before I had an accident. I shut my eyes in a vain effort to make the spinning stop. I could feel the world tilt even as I laid still on my beat up old mattress. I timed my breathing and little by little I regained control. I kicked my shoes off and flipped some covers over my body. It was late and there was not much more I could do tonight. Tomorrow was a new day.

When I came to the next morning, my skull felt as if an axe had been embedded in it, not a particularly good feeling. I rolled out of bed and reached for my phone, and I began to listen. The first voicemail was from my sister, drunk dialing her little brother at midnight. That is the only normal one out of the two messages I had. The other one was from my father.

Dad and I are on acceptable terms. He accepts that I am a failure and continuously reminds me of it. I accept that he is a prick who never took the time to understand his son. To be fair there is love; it's just mucked up with plenty of crossed wires. Our main problem is he doesn't support my goals. He believes this to be some phase I will grow out of and then go work in an office basement somewhere, to become just another cog in the machine. There was a certain way we acted around each other, and there was much unsaid.

When I heard what he was saying, there was none of his usual tone. Dad sounded genuinely concerned. He was speaking of the news of some rogue signal that carried a doomsday warning. He was talking so fast that I could barely understand what he was saying. I went to my computer and opened up the home page. It was splashed across every site. Though there was a lack of concrete information, it didn't stop the conspiracy theorists from adding fuel to the fire. The government had "no comment."

"Aaron," Dad said. "You need to come home now."

My parents lived just fifteen miles out of town, tucked away in a rural area. They moved there after Sandra and I went out on our own. It's quite smaller than the place we lived in before, but at their age they don't need much. Hell, if my dad could stand sleeping on a cot, he would just live in the garage. He practically does now.

As I pulled up the gravel driveway, I could see that my sister had already arrived. Sandra was a dichotomy; more responsible than me, but more dependent on our parents. She called the house all the time. Like several times a day. I joked with Dad that he may not like my choices, but at least I'm more self sufficient. I believe he secretly agrees with me on that.

As I walked through the screen door, the place was unbearably quiet, as if I was attending a wake. I found the three of them in the kitchen. Sandra was crying. My parents remained stoic.

"Hey guys," I said.

"Aaron," Mom said, getting up to hug me.

"Hi Mom," I said.

"I take you got my message," Dad said.

"I did. Is this real?" I asked.

"No one's commenting," he said. "But it looks like it."

I swallowed hard. It's amazing how everything can be rendered meaningless by a ticking clock. All the progress humanity has made, voided like an afterthought.

"Do they know when?" I asked Dad.

"Sunday; they don't know the exact time."

"What are you going to do?"

"There's not much we can do," he said. "Your sister is going to stay with us. We'd like you to come too."

It should've been an easy answer. I should've said yes. I would move in for the last few days and we would spend time together and reminisce. Be reminded how fragile life is and how much we didn't say we loved each other.

Something prevented me from doing that. As selfish as it was, all I could think about was how little I had accomplished in life. The idea of it being over with nothing to show for it did not sit well with me. I was going to finish what I started, or die trying.

"I wish I could Dad," I said.

"What?" he said shocked at my answer.

"I need to go home," I said, heading for the door. "I need to write."

I didn't even make it off the porch before my father caught me.

"Aaron. Wait up," he said.

"I'm sorry Dad. I need to do this," I said.

"You could write here," he said.

"I need to be away from here," I replied.

"What's that supposed to mean?"

"I didn't mean it like that. Dad, let's not fight."

"Son, don't do this."

"Dad, it's not like I'm not coming back. I'll come home for dinner every night for a few hours. Spend time with you, Mom, and with Sandra."

"You can't abandon your family," he said.

"I'm not—"I began but he cut me off.

"All for a stupid dream," he said his voice soaked with bitterness.

That pissed me off to put it mildly. My eyes narrowed into daggers and I seriously considered hitting him. My better judgment stopped me. The last thing I needed to be thinking about was sucker punching Dad.

"Don't belittle what I want," I said. "This is important to me. It always has been important to me. You never tried to understand it. You never had any faith in it."

"In you, yes. Not in your writing. You've been trying for years. Look what it has gotten you, nothing."

"Dad," I said, trying to find the words I should've said a long time ago. "I've always been told that I should do what makes me happy. Well, this is it. Writing makes me happy. I'm going to finish a novel. You'll see."

I turned and walked to my car. I hesitated at the driver's door. I knew he would say something else.

"Aaron," he said. I looked back up. His expression was a mixture of resignation and sorrow. "Nothing's going to survive this. You'll be doing it for nothing. It's not going to matter."

"That's where you're wrong," I said. "It'll matter to me."

When I got back to my apartment, I was pissed off. The last thing I wanted was to spend my last three days hating my father. All I wanted was to prove that I could do it. Why was that so horrible? I didn't understand it.

Time was of the essence, so I cleaned my apartment. A clear work space made for a clear mind. The fewer distractions I had the better. After that was done, I powered up the computer and I opened up a new word document. The cursor was back again, blinking away, but this time I was ready.

Normally, I would start by just writing and see if I could find a plot in the middle of it all, but since this would be my only shot, I wanted to think it out some. When it came to an idea, I decided to be topical and what better topic to write about than the impending apocalypse? That was one thing I definitely knew about.

I was experiencing the stark realization that I was not going to live to see my twenty seventh birthday. Everything was going to be destroyed, taken from me, from all of us in a blink of an eye. So that was what I would write about.

James Sunder should have died.
Like the others.
His life had been spared by chance. James had gone down into the bunker to check the inventory for his father. His father, to put it mildly, was a bit paranoid, always on a cusp of a meltdown. James' father was certain that the end was near.

James was not concerned by these views. Outside the bomb shelter and the occasional doomsday rant, his dad was just like anyone else. It was a strange way to spend one's money, but as James saw it, if people loved to splurge on automobiles and The Home Shopping Network then more power to his dad. This was his passion. He should be allowed to follow it no matter how deranged it looked, besides, he wasn't hurting anyone.

The bunker was a good twenty feet underground accessible by a steel ladder. The entrance to the bunker was a sturdy one, several inches of thick steel with a spinning wheel for its locking mechanism. The room itself was the size of a two bedroom apartment. It had all the amenities of home plus enough food to feed several people, a small family for at least six months.

James moved from room to room, ticking off the items on his clipboard and their numeric counts. Four hundred bottles clean drinking water. Check. Twenty large boxes of strike anywhere matches. Check. Enough ready to eat meals to feed several platoons. Check and double check. His father had wanted an accurate count in order to decide how much more supplies he was going to purchase. James was so wrapped up in the task at hand that he almost didn't hear the first bomb go off.

A knock at the door pulled me out of work. I checked the clock in the corner of the screen. Five hours had passed and I had close to ten thousand words. My hands ached and cracking my knuckles did little to alleviate the pain. I hit the save button and went to see who it was. I needed a break as is.

I found my neighbor Krista in the doorway. Krista lived two doors down. I had always thought she was beautiful; she was five foot something, normal for a girl, with jet black shoulder length hair and hazel eyes that always seemed to be hiding something. She was thin but not in an anorexic sense and I could tell she was toned. Outside of idle chit chat however, we rarely talked. I knew little about her, so I instead guessed what I could. I guess it was the writer in me; we're always mindful of the details.

Details like her eclectic taste in clothing. Weird as it was, I always noticed the type of shoes she wore. My favorite of hers was a pair of bright white sneakers with pink laces. I can't explain why, but I felt happy whenever I saw she was wearing them. Perhaps it was because they complimented whatever she was wore, which in turn complimented her own beauty.

None of this however, mattered. I couldn't act on my attraction because I was still with Rebecca at the time and cheating was not in my blood. As it were, Krista seemed to have her shit together. There was no way she'd be into me.

Or so I thought.

"Hi," she said.

"Hi," I said back. I wondered why she came to see me. We were friendly to each other, but we weren't friends per se. We would say hello in the hallway and converse about the weather, but that was about it. Yet, here she was at my apartment.

"Can I come in?" she asked.

"Sure," I said, opening the door wider for her to enter. She took a look around and nodded in approval.

"Nice place," she said.

"Thanks," I replied.

"How can you afford this?"

"I sell drugs," I joked. "Writing has yet to pay the bills."

She politely laughed. "I guess it never will."

"So you've heard."

"Hasn't everyone?"

"True," I said. "How do you feel?"

"I don't know how I feel," she said. "I feel..." Krista began then let it hang. She couldn't find the words. I could relate.

"Feel what?" I asked.

"I feel all this regret." she said, pacing the room. "All these things I haven't done that I should have. Places I didn't go. People I didn't fuck."

I smirked and arched an eyebrow. "A little forward aren't we? Don't you think you should at least buy me dinner first?"

Krista laughed and hit me on the shoulder. "Shut up."

"Just saying," I replied with false modesty.

"You would. I'm just saying, no one dies thinking, 'God I shouldn't have fucked so much. Sex is fun, feels good. You should know Aaron. I bet you broke some hearts in your day."

I shook my head. "Mostly the other way around, actually," I said.

"Poor baby."

"I manage."

There was a lull in the conversation. I was trying to figure out what was going on. I've never had a woman be so upfront with her sexual proclivities before.

"Let's test a theory of mine," Krista said, breaking the silence.

"What theory?" I asked.

"Kiss me."

"Excuse me?"

"Come on don't be a pussy," she said.

I inched closer to her. "I don't see what this is going to prove."

"I want to see what type of kisser you are," she said. "I think you're a heartbreaker. I want to see if I'm right."

"Okay," I said.

"Just fucking do it," she said.

"Fine," I said. I grabbed her at the waist and just went for it, giving her what she wanted. It was supposed to be a quick kiss, seven seconds or so. But she wasn't breaking away. Neither was I, I felt a familiar stirring, one I had admittedly not felt for Rebecca in quite some time.

The kiss finally broke, mainly for our mutual need of air. Krista sucked it in, panting.

"Damn," she said.

"Yeah," I replied between breaths.

"I hate being right."

"What?"

"I have a confession to make," she said.

"Okay," I said.

"I came over for a reason."

Our eyes locked. I kissed her again, hard, pulling her body tightly to mine. I reached for her shirt and pulled it over her head with ease. Her breasts were shapely, the nipples aroused, the size of small pebbles. She went for my pants buckle and proceeded to undo it. Rational thought was quickly leaving my mind.

"We don't have to do this...if you know you don't want to," I said, words tumbling out. Smooth I was not.

"Shh..." she said, kissing me with tongue. At this point I was at full attention and in no condition to argue.

"You're over thinking it," she said, as she snaked her jeans down to her ankles. "Don't. Now take off your pants."

After we were done, Krista and I shared a cigarette. It had been several years since I had quit, but I was a dead man anyway so fuck it.

"Should we talk about what the hell just happened?" I asked.

"All I know is you made me hurt so good, Mmm," Krista said, smiling. "I'm going to be sore tomorrow because of you."

"That makes two of us," I said. "How did you learn to do that thing with your back?"

"Practice," she said with a devilish grin. "Plenty of practice."

"I see."

"Can I ask you a question?" she asked.

"Ask away," I replied.

"Why aren't you with your family?"

"That requires another cigarette. Do you have one?"

"Sure," she said.

Krista handed me one and I lit it, taking a drag.

"I want to finish writing a novel before I die. I've tried for years and gotten nowhere. I don't want to die a failure. I don't want to have things to regret either."

She nodded. "I take your parents, most likely your dad, don't support it?"

"Yeah," I said. "I've tried to explain to him what it means to me but he doesn't get it. He thinks I'm just trying to piss him off."

"Maybe you are," she said.

"I love my family, Kris. But I have to do this. It is really important to me."

"Then he should support you. Even if he doesn't outwardly show it," she replied.

Krista reached for her clothes, hastily dressing. I followed her to the door, clad only in blue jeans. The whole past hour had been a surreal occurrence for the both of us; primal lust at its finest.

"I'd stay," she said. "But I have matters to attend to. Besides, I don't want to side track you any further. You've got a story to finish, novelist."

"That I do," I said.

"Do you want to come by tomorrow night?" she asked with a sly look."We could drink some wine, commiserate, and you know have some more fun."

There was no way in hell I would pass that up.

"That would be great," I said nonchalantly.

"Good. Say ten?"

"Optimal."

"All right then," Krista said, planting a quick peck on my cheek. "Later stud."

When James heard the first blast, he didn't realize what it was. When he heard the second and third blasts, James knew something was wrong. He hadn't locked the door so he tore down the walkway till he reached the ladder. He climbed quickly, skipping two rungs at a time.

When he reached the top, James could not comprehend what his eyes were showing him. The sky, which had been a clear light blue, was now a dark black color. He could see mushroom clouds in the distance that reached high as the heavens. James could not be certain if the blasts were nuclear, but he wouldn't stick around to find out. The thing with nuclear weapons is the initial blast wasn't what you need to be worried about.

It was the fallout.

It was close to dinner time, so I headed to my parent's. I knew Dad was still a bit sore about our blow up earlier, but he'd get over it. He'd have to. I wasn't planning on abandoning them. I would spend as much time with them as I could spare. We would still be a family.

Mom answered the door when I knocked. She said nothing, leading me silently into the kitchen. They were just about to eat dinner. Grilled chicken with rice and corn on the cob. Dad and Sandra were already sitting, bowing their heads to say grace. I quickly did the same. After a minute they were done, and I took it as my signal that it was okay to dig in. I consumed the food quickly because I was ravished with hunger. Writing is more strenuous than it looks. It takes quite a bit out of you.

"The drive here okay?" Mom asked.

"It was no problem actually," I said. "There was no one on the road. It was odd."

Mom nodded. "I see," she said.

"How's the book coming?" Sandra asked.

"It's going well," I said.

"I hope it's worth it son," Dad said in his best stern voice.

"It is," I replied back icily.

The dinner table got real quiet after that. There wasn't much else to talk about. If this was any other day, Sandra would be complaining about her latest boyfriend. Dad would be ranting about an engine part that wouldn't stop breaking and Mom would be boring us about her latest book club meeting. None of these things were discussed, for they no longer mattered. What we thought had value didn't. This was no longer just any day.

It was the Last Days.

After the table was cleared, Sandra and Mom retired to the den. Dad went to his garage, mumbling about fixing something. Hedging my bets, I decided to follow Sandra and Mom. I found them on the living room floor, flipping through a photo album, pointing and laughing.

"Do you remember this one Aaron?" Sandra asked, pointing to a photo of me when I was two. "You had the bike stuck on a curb and couldn't dislodge it."

"You went 'Pick it up! Pick it up!'" Mom said laughing.

"Pick it up!" Sandra echoed.

I had to grin. I had seen the family video of this incident so I couldn't deny that it occurred. It is amazing what they remembered. I don't remember much of my childhood. It comes back to me in a collective blur, fragments really, some good, most bad. Part of the reason I couldn't remember was because I was actively trying to forget it. The parts I could recall seemed unreal, as I hadn't lived them.

Sandra's phone rang in the middle of our reminiscing. She looked at the caller I.D. and frowned.

"It's Brian," she said. "I have to take this."

"Go ahead," Mom said. "We'll be here."

Sandra headed upstairs to talk in private. I sat by Mom while she made comments on every photo. Her ability to remember them all was astounding.

"How do you remember these things?" I asked her.

"It's a Mother's job to remember," she said.

"Yeah, but still..."

"I guess I'm just good with details."

I accepted the statement at face value. Mom was always on top of things. Whether it was important dates, boyfriends and girlfriends, successes and failures, she kept it all. It was a wonder she able to have a life of her own.

"Your father loves you," she said gingerly. We never talked about the relationship between Dad and me but she knew. She'd have to be blind to not know.

"I know," I said.

"He just wants you to be here."

"I understand that, but I need to do this."

"He knows that."

"He has a hell of a way of showing it," I said.

"I know, but the men of this family always hold their cards close to the chest. Your father is no different. He's always believed in you, even now. Never question that."

"I understand," I said.

"I hope you do," she said.

"So," I began, trying to change the subject. "Brian is Sandra's latest boyfriend?"

"Yes," Mom said, smiling sadly. "She met three weeks ago. It was the epitome of bad timing."

"Indeed," I said.

"What about you? Met any cute girls?"

"Well, I spent some time with my neighbor today. Krista."

"What do you two do?" Mom asked.

"We talked," I said.

I didn't get home until after eleven. I had no intention of sleeping. I couldn't afford the time. My novel was coming along, but I would have to accept the bare minimum of rest in order to finish it. Come to think it, I don't think anyone would be sleeping. They would want to have every possible second to themselves.

In any case, I had a secret weapon to combat exhaustion for a few hours at least. When regular coffee just wouldn't cut it, I had a small espresso machine to pick up the slack. I brewed myself two cups. It was going to be one of those nights. I might as well be realistic.

James slid down the ladder like a sailor and ran for the bunker door. He slammed it hard, his survival instinct kicking in. He spun the wheel lock until it clanked shut. James knew his folks were still out there, but his father would never want him to jeopardize his own safety. Besides, James thought, his father would know to come down with Mom. When they knocked on the door, he would open up in a heartbeat. Dad would be there any second now.

James pulled up a chair next to the entrance and waited. He sat attentively, listening for the smallest of noises. A couple times James could've sworn he heard knocking. Dad would've yelled something. He would've made a much louder bang with his fist. So he waited. He waited hours for a sign of life.

And yet, no one knocked.

My alarm woke me up at exactly seven a.m. I felt tired, but I couldn't bitch. The clock was ticking. Unfortunately, my body functioned with the dexterity of a re-animated corpse. Ten minutes under scalding water would hopefully bring some spring back into my step.

The shower made me relaxed, but it did little for my lucidity. So while I was unwinding my muscles, I let the coffee pot do its magic. After I dried off, I attacked the first cup like a fat kid denied candy for a week. A few cups later and I was fine. With enough caffeine in your blood stream you can do anything.

I spent some time online to see if I could gleam any new information about what was going on. I found nothing of worth, just the same generalized facts. There was no consensus. It bothered me, but I pushed these worries from my mind. I had no time for it. I had a job to do, one I intended on completing.

The next few days went by in a blur for James Sunder. He spent most of his time at the bunker door, hoping to hear his father, or anyone who was still alive. He listened to the radio, twisting the dials, but got nothing but static. James ate little for he had no appetite.

When James dreamed, he dreamed of fire. Of cities destroyed to rubble and his love ones melting as he stood nearby, helpless to alleviate their pain. James didn't sleep much after that. He was already living a nightmare and he didn't need to be reminded of it every time he closed his eyes.

To pass the time, James read. His father had stocked shelves all around the bunker walls with literature. His father once told him that books were important as words enriched the soul. James tackled every scrap of literature with furor. Anything to keep his mind off the things he did, or rather didn't do.

Unfortunately, that could only hold him over for so long. His mind began to wander again. He would map out scenarios in his head. The questions were the worst part. They plagued him incessantly. Why did this happen? Was their town the only place affected by the bombs? Was everyone dead? The most sobering thought was being the last man, the last person alive in the world. James tried to not think of that one; it would drive him mad.

Those were how his days went; routine then more routine. He would spend time at the door, listening for signs of life. He would exercise. He would eat. He'd listen to static on the radio. He would read, then cap off the night feigning sleep and cleanliness. Every night

*when he closed his eyes, James prayed he
wasn't the only one left in the world, and when
he rejoined it, he hoped he'd still have his
sanity intact to embrace it.*

I returned to my parents on Saturday
night for dinner. It was tense. We had nothing
to say, but everything to think about. The food
was passed around the table in grave silence
and we gave curt responses to one another.
There wasn't a pulse to the proceedings.
Reality had sunk in.
This was it.
This was all that would be.
Not exactly fodder for a robust
conversation.
After dinner Mom and Dad left us to
our own devices. Sandra and I took residence
in the living room. We sat on opposite sides of
the room and didn't say much.
"Have you talked to Brian?" I asked.
She nodded. "I'm going to call him later.
See him tonight."
"Good."
"I love him," Sandra blurted out
unexpectedly.
"You do?" was all I could say.
"Yes. Yes, I do. I think," she said.
"Don't say it if you don't mean it," I
cautioned her.
Sandra stayed silent for a long time.
"I just want to love someone," she
finally confessed. "Be loved by someone. Is
that so wrong?"
"No," I replied. "No it isn't."

"Have you ever been in love Aaron?" she asked.

"I guess," I said.

"You guess?"

"I've loved many girls but few ever felt the same way."

"What about Rebecca? Didn't you love her?"

"I did, but we just couldn't make it work. Your brother was too much of a fuck up."

"Indeed. What about that neighbor of yours?" she asked.

"Who told you about her?" I asked defensively.

"Mom," she said.

"Krista? We're just enjoying each other's company."

"You slept with her didn't you," Sandra said, her face scrunching up.

"I plead the fifth on that," I said.

"Eww. I didn't need to know."

The air conditioning kicked on and the hair on my arms stood up. The clock on the nearby table clicked away another minute, unmoved by our plight. Sandra breathed deep and sighed.

"It's getting late," she said to no one. "We don't have much time."

I took that as my cue to leave.

"I'll see you at breakfast," I said, "I'll be done then."

James Sunder was out of time.
He was certain.

Food was running out as the stress of his situation had led him to overeat. He had lost track of time, unsure of how long he had been underground. His mind was playing tricks on him, making him see and hear things that weren't there. His mind was all he had left. It would be the last thing to go.

James never did find a single radio signal despite all his searching. There was no contact with the outside world. He hadn't spoken to another person in so long. It was eating away at him. It would only be a matter of time before he started to rant at inanimate objects.

James had only one other option. It was more of a "Sophie's Choice" really. His father ever the paranoid one, had placed something other than food and water inside the bunker walls. Unbeknownst to James, his father had also procured several Hazmat suits. The kind used to protect somewhat against radioactivity. He was even able to procure a Geiger counter to check for radioactivity. James didn't know how his father got them or how much he must've paid.

James knew only one thing. If he stayed, he would die. There was no getting around that, but the suit wasn't designed for full on exposure. If he found himself in a spot where the radiation was too great it would seep through the suit and kill him in a slow and painful manner. It would be an unthinkable fate.

He thought it over. It was worth the risk. It was better to take a chance for life rather than play it safe for death.

He was going to surface.

It was close to nine-thirty p.m. when I finished up my second to last session. I was almost done and all I needed was the ending. The jury was still out on that though. I'd worry about it when I got back. I had a "date."

I knocked on Krista's door and waited. It took several moments before she finally answered. It was well worth the wait. When she opened the door she was wearing a simple blue dress, but it accentuated the perfections of her figure. God bless the designer.

"Hi," I said.

"Hi," she said back.

I handed her a bottle of wine that I brought.

"This is for you," I said.

"A guest who brings gifts," she said. "Come on in."

Her place was quite cleaner than mine. One thing I did notice was her walls were covered top to bottom in art. On closer inspection, I realized that most of it was hers. She was a painter.

"You're an artist?" I asked.

She shrugged. "I guess I forgot to mention that."

"Ever sell any of them?"

"No."

"Then how do you afford your place?"

"My trust fund and occasional forays into prostitution," she said with a straight face.

"Mom must be proud," I joked.

"She is, ever so," Krista deadpanned.

I moved into the kitchen where Krista opened the bottle. She reached for two glasses and begun to fill them.

"I have to ask something," I said.

"Go ahead," Krista replied.

"What exactly are we doing here?"

She stopped mid pour. "What do you mean?"

"I mean everything that happened in the past day."

Krista finished pouring and started to drink from hers. Three quick sips and her first glass was gone. She placed it back down on the marble counter.

"Let's just say we're two souls, connecting for a time," Krista said. She pointed to my glass. "Aren't you going to drink that?"

I hastily brought it to my lips and drank half of it.

"That's the spirit, Hemingway," she said. "Have you enjoyed my company?"

"Very much so," I said, finishing the glass. "And you?"

"Another confession if I may?" she asked.

"Go ahead," I said.

"I always thought you were cute. Almost tried to steal you from that girlfriend of yours, but I didn't. Maybe I should have. Who knows what would've happened."

I didn't know what to say. I did the next logical thing.

"Do you want another glass?" I asked.

"Desperately," she sighed.

We made love that night. It was a more subdued affair then our previous rendezvous. Krista wanted me to go slow and I had no objections. As I moved on top of her, she made soft little panting noises that drove me to the point of madness. Her hands gripped the back of my neck, holding me closer. The room was deathly quiet outside of our heavy breathing and I felt sweat trickle down my back. I looked into her eyes and felt the indescribable. Perhaps a connection akin to the one Sandra claimed to have for her boyfriend. I kissed her neck and she moaned into my ear as our tempo increased. Our climax was simultaneous, our bodies locked together in a feeling that might never be ours again.

Krista clasped onto my chest, her head resting on my stomach. I smoked a cigarette.

"Bum a smoke?" Krista asked, sitting back up next to me.

"Sure," I said, handing it over. She took several drags before handing it back. I finished it and jabbed what was left in the ashtray.

"Are you scared?" I asked.

Her expression said it all.

"I'm terrified. I'm going to die alone," she said.

"No you're not," I said.

"Yes, I am. I have no one to face this with."

"What about you parents?"

"My parent's idea of love is a monthly check. They're in Europe, I think, the bastards," Krista said, anger creeping into her voice. She sighed. "I'm going to die and no one will care."

"I'll care," I said.

She smiled ever so slightly.

"Thank you," she said. "That means something to me."

It was getting late and she was drifting off. It would only be minutes before she would be lost to dreams.

"Will you stay with me until I fall asleep?" she asked.

"Of course," I said.

"Going to finish your book tonight?"

"I have to."

"Good luck," she said. "Send me a copy. I'd like to read it in the morning. That is if we have time."

"I'll do that."

"It's been fun," she said.

"Yes it has," I replied.

After Krista fell asleep I snuck out of her apartment and back into mine. I had no time to rest; I had a book to finish. I powered up the computer for the final time and opened up my novel. Glorious words stared back at me, the fruits of strenuous labor. It would all be for naught if I did not finish. The ending was crucial. It had to be perfect.

A few hours ago, I had no clue on how to finish the story. After a night with Krista however, I knew the solution to my problem. I knew how to end it. I placed my fingers to the keys and began to type, running my final sprint.

It was now Sunday, and supposedly the beginning of the end. Whatever you wanted to call it, it was here, and yet no one knew how it would come. I imagined that world leaders were off in steel bunkers somewhere vainly trying to escape it. There was no running from this though.

I stretched and moved over to my laptop. I decided on the title *Beginnings* for my novel. It seemed liked the perfect fit. I had printed out three copies the night before to take to with me. One was for Sandra and Mom. One was for Krista. The other one was for Dad.

I knocked hard on Krista's door. I could hear a shuffling of feet and the door swung open. Krista rubbed her eyes hard.

"Aaron? What are you doing here?" she asked, yawning.

"Get dressed. I'm taking you to breakfast. You can meet my family," I said.

"I beg your pardon?"

"Nobody should be alone, Kris. Now you don't have to be."

She grinned, exhaustion leaving her.

"Okay," she said. "Give me ten minutes."

The drive was uneventful. We were the only car on the road. It was disquieting actually, to be the only apparent sign of life.

"Did you finish it?" Krista asked.

I reached into the back seat and pulled out one of the copies. "See for yourself."

Krista began to read as I paid attention to the road. There might not be people to reckon with, but a stray deer could still cross the road.

"You wrote the entire thing in three days?" Krista asked disbelieving.

"Yep," I replied casually.

"You're insane, you know that?"

"Clinically."

When we arrived at the house, my family was out on the porch, most likely taking in the sun for the last time. When they saw Krista, they looked bemused. I never talked about my personal life much.

"You brought a friend?" Mom asked.

"Mom, Dad, Sandra, this is Krista. Krista, this is my family," I said.

"Hello," Krista said.

"Hi dear," Mom said.

"Hi," Sandra said.

Dad just nodded.

Mom went all out for breakfast. Whatever you can think of, we had the option to eat it. I could barely move afterwards. We left the dishes piled in the sink because, well, we didn't have to worry about washing them.

As Dad retired to the garage, I joined Mom, Sandra, and Krista in the living room. I didn't intend to stay long. I handed one of the copies of my book to Mom.

"I finished it." I said, "I'm gonna find Dad, okay?"

Mom nodded, understanding.

To no surprise I found him in the garage, tinkering with a lawn mower engine. His hands were covered with grease, and apparently at some point he had nicked himself, and I noticed a small trickle of blood.

"Hours to go and you need to make sure the lawnmower works," I said.

Dad looked up and gave me a "who knows" shrug.

"Keeps my mind off things," he said.

"Get your hands clean. I'll take a look," I said.

Dad went to the sink and used some hand cleaner to remove the mess. I waited patiently as he scrubbed at every nook and cranny.

"So did you sleep with her?" Dad asked.

"I beg your pardon?" I asked shocked.

"I'm just asking."

"If you must know, yes I did, twice."

"That's my boy," Dad said, chuckling. He shut the water off and gingerly dried his hands.

"Now what?" he asked.

I handed him the manuscript. His expression said it all.

"Now you read," I said. "Don't worry, it's not that long. I thought you should see it once though."

Dad nodded and found himself a chair in the corner while I hit the floor to figure out the problem with the engine. I wasn't a mechanical wiz like Dad but he taught me a thing or two. I knew my way around a toolbox. It took two hours of trial and error, but I finally got the thing put back together. I changed the oil and added fuel. I gave the cord a tug and it roared to life. I smiled then shut it back off.

"Good thing I had a hell of a teacher," I said to Dad, but he was too busy to listen.

He was on the last page of *Beginnings*.

I waited there until he was done. When he flipped the last page closed, he looked up at me and gave me a smile. The "I'm proud" smile you rarely see from your parents.

"It's good," he said.

The first thing that caught James Sunder off guard was the sky.

The sun was out.

That troubled him. In everything he read on nuclear fallout that was not normal. Fallout would've caused acid rain and ash to fall from the sky, but the sky was clear. Perhaps it was not nuclear. James was not convinced yet. He wasn't going to take off the suit based off a hunch, even a positive one. He had to be sure.

James pulled out the Geiger counter and flicked it on. It crackled to life, letting out some static. There was nothing to be worried about yet, but this was not a confirmation of safety either. He would have to canvass more of the area.

Looking straight ahead, he saw his house no longer stood. Only scarce debris remained. Relief hit him, even though it was horrible to feel it. The shock blast from the bombs must've destroyed the house shortly after detonation. His parents couldn't have gotten out of the blast zone even if they had wanted to. Guilt no longer plagued him. There was nothing he could've done. It was not his fault.

James begin to walk, testing areas for radiation. He found a few pockets, but nothing that would constitute life threatening. Perhaps the brunt of the damage had stayed at the point of detonation. He hoped for as much. He kept his suit on though.

Better safe than sorry.

The sun was about to set when out the corner of his eye James swore he saw something or rather someone. They had seen him first and darted back behind a large pile of debris in the distance. James ran as fast as his heavy suit would allow him, hoping he was not going mad. That he was not alone.

He found the person in question cowering in a ball on the ground, obstinately trying to hide from him. When he placed his hand on the person's shoulder, they jumped up with fright, backpedaling with every step. Finally getting a good look, James saw it was not a man but rather a young woman.

She had seen better days, but then again, so had everyone else. Her long brown hair was matted to her skull and was in dire need of shampoo. Her clothes were torn and ragged. It was quite possible that she had been wearing them for months. James noticed this, but paid them no real attention. He was focused on something else.

Beyond the dirt and grime, the girl had piercing hazel eyes. They struck him dead center and in them he saw all he needed to know. He saw her pain, her confusion, her will to survive. She was scared and perhaps he could help her.

"Stay away from me," she pleaded, catching him off guard. "Don't come any closer."

James tried to say "I'm not going to hurt you." However, his voice was muffled by the suit. The best he could do was random arm flaying. He took a step closer and she yelped.

"Stay back!" she screamed, turning to run.

She moved at a fast clip. James was initially impressed, but realized a big problem. He would not be able to catch her in the suit. He made a split decision right there. A stupid one, but it had to be done. He quickly tore it off and ran off after her.

"Wait," he called out when he was in sprinting distance of her. She turned to look back and saw James, not the hulking mass in a hazmat suit. She slowed down to a crawl, trying desperately to catch her breath.

"Who are you?" she asked.

"I was the guy back there in the suit," James said.

"Oh," she replied, her eyes darting for another escape.

"I'm not going to hurt you," James said quickly to keep her from running again. "The suit was for protection, which I apparently don't need. Do you know what happened here?"

The girl shook her head.

"I know as much as you do," she said.

"Okay," James said breathing deep. "Let's start again shall we? I'm James and you are?"

"Kate," she said. "What do you want?"

"I haven't seen a soul in months. I needed to be sure I wasn't alone."

They walked together back to where James had stripped off the suit. He left it on the ground (he had a few spares in the bunker) but retrieved the Geiger counter just in case. The area was relatively safe but the last thing they wanted to do was walk into the wrong area without warning.

"How did you survive?" Kate asked him.

"I was doing inventory for my dad. He had an underground bunker. Right place, right time," James said. "What about you?"

"I was in the basement with my grandfather and we held up there. He died about a week ago, natural causes."

"I'm sorry."

"Earlier, I was scared. When I saw you in the suit, I just thought one thing."

"That you were a goner," James said.

"Yeah," Kate said.

"Who knows," James said bitterly. "We still might be."

They returned to bunker just before nightfall. James led her down. He told her that it was only temporary. James only had a few days' supplies left and after that they would need a game plan.

"There's still plenty of water for the shower, if you'd like one," James said.

"I'd kill for one," Kate said.

"No killing necessary," James said, throwing his hands up in mock surrender. "Go on ahead. There are some fresh clothes in the closet as well. You probably would want those too."

Kate closed the door to the bathroom but it kicked back an inch. James knew it was wrong, but he couldn't resist looking. It was just a guy's nature. She had a nice body. James hadn't been with a woman in a long time and old stirrings began to awaken inside him. James ignored them and began to do inventory of what was left. He needed to give the poor girl some privacy.

After she cleaned up, James gave her some food from the dwindling stash. She ate ravenously.

"That was delicious," Kate said, taking a final swallow.

"You're welcome," James said.

"So...what's the plan?"

"Well, we can spend another day here. Get some rest and everything. Afterwards, we should head out and see if we can find somewhere that wasn't affected. Find other people. Live on. You know the simple stuff."

Kate scoffed. "You make it seem like it will be easy."

"It won't," James said with firmness. "But if we stay here, we die, plain and simple."

Kate began to cry. James didn't know what to do. Perhaps he was too harsh. He reached for her hand.

"Hey," he said. "I didn't mean to scare you. But that's the facts at hand. We need to get out here. Find a place away from this mess. We're going to be okay."

"You're sure?" Kate asked.

"I'm positive. If we can survive this, we can survive anything," James said.

They were still holding hands. She had not pulled hers away. In fact, she seemed to grip a little tighter. They looked at each other and James felt a connection with the woman sitting across from him. It was not sexual, this feeling; it was something else entirely. In that moment James smiled. He could not remember the last time he had done that. Together underneath the ground and the flickering fluorescent lights illuminating them, they had hope.

There was hope.

ERIC

People assume because I'm a priest I have all the answers. I don't. I have very few actually. Just because I speak for God does not mean I can explain it all. That's a danger of the job. Everyone wants that clear cut answer. The one that makes their problem magically disappear. I try to remind people that when one problem is solved, two usually pop up in its place. So is the way of life.

Don't get it twisted. I'm not a cynic. I believe in what I do. I'm just realistic about it. The world is complicated. Everybody desires answers, everybody wants the truth. Most of us don't get it and contrary to popular belief, my job is not about the answers. My job is to give advice and guidance. I can point you in the right direction, but you have to find the answers for yourself. You must choose your path. Salvation rests in your hands.

As priests, we know that confession is by far one of our most important duties. Priests are glad to offer absolution. We are happy people come to us. It shows they have remorse. It shows they're not perfect and perhaps want to change. The church embraces that.

While most of what I hear is of the mundane variety, a very small of percentage keeps me up at night. Confession can also be the place where the unrepentant come to gloat. I've lost count the number of times over the years when I have been privy to heinous acts. Through a mesh window, I can tell they have no remorse in what they have done. They will sin again. They tell me because they are compelled to tell someone and what better man than the one who can never divulge their secrets?

I sit there and listen as my fellow man spills malevolence from their lips as afterthoughts. They search through the window for a reaction. I put on a front of composure and discuss redemption. They pretend to listen. I set a penance that is mostly frivolous and suggest that they answer for what they've done. They don't of course, and walk out empowered by the lack of actual punishment for their transgressions. They bask in the knowledge that their secrets are safe. In one moment, I see humanity at its darkest, and there is nothing I can do about it.

We all like to think that evil is punished by God. That no one escapes judgment. Now I'm not so sure. Everything seems grey. People seem to go unpunished all the time. Some are even celebrated for it. It's unjust, but it's the way things are. I wish it wasn't so, but it's not my job to fix it. My life is one of service, to people and to God. Even if I was tasked with solving the problems, I wouldn't know where to begin. The dam has already burst; we're just waiting to drown.

It was late Thursday evening and I was doing the last rounds of confession. The day had been uneventful, with a sparsely attended service and some office duties. I was tired, and looking forward to a good night's sleep. I yawned loudly, getting it out of my system before someone came in. I rubbed my eyes and gave myself a few light taps to the face. I was ready.

The door opened and I adjusted my posture in the seat. I glanced at the screen that separated us and I waited for them to speak.

"Bless me Father, for I have sinned. It has been five years since my last confession," A woman said.

"Go on," I said.

"I've done terrible things. I've hurt people emotionally, played with the feelings of others. I didn't care. I thought nothing of it. 'People just needed to toughen up.' I thought. That was me denying what I'd done."

"I understand," I said.

"I want to be a better person before it is too late."

"So few of us can be honest and recognize our flaws. It's good you came to me."

"I have many things to make amends for," she sighed. "The time I have left, it's so fleeting..."

"What do you mean, my child?" I asked, not understanding.

"Haven't you heard?"

"Heard what?"

I heard the woman gasp.

"Father," she said. "You really don't know?"

"Know what?" I said.

"It's all over the news."

"What is?"

"The world," she said, her voice becoming a low whisper. "It's about to end."

I remained silent for several minutes after she said that, waiting for her to laugh, to snicker. To show any sign that she wasn't actually serious. I didn't get one.

"Father, are you okay?" she asked, concerned.

"I'm fine," I said. "Are you sure of what you're telling me?"

"It's everywhere. All the news channels have been reporting on it. Every government has been silent on the issue. They're trying to play it off but no one believes them."

"And rightly so, my child; they deny it for it has no basis in fact."

"What about the Pope?" she asked.

"What about him?"

"He made a statement tonight from Rome. He says the world must join together in prayer to save us from impending doom. Why would he say that if there is no truth to this?"

Whatever color I still had in my face drained. "I see," I said, even though I didn't.

"I'm sorry you had to find out this way," she said.

"This isn't your fault," I replied. "How long do we have?"

"They say it will happen Sunday. They don't know when."

"I see."

"Father?"

"Yes?"

"In regards to what I talked about," she said.

Her confession, right, I almost forgot.

"For you penance, say three Hail Mary's and an Our Father; in addition, you must make amends to those you have hurt," I said.

"I understand, Father."

""God, the Father of Mercy through the Death and Resurrection of His Son has reconciled the world to Himself and sent the Holy Spirit among us for the forgiveness of sins. By the ministry of the Church, may God grant you pardon and peace and I absolve you of your sins in the Name of the Father, and of the Son, and of the Holy Spirit. Go in peace, your sins have been forgiven."

"Thank you Father."

"One more thing," I noted.

"Yes?"

"If there is any truth to this, do not squander the time God has given you. Use it wisely."

"I will."

"Go with God, my child. Now if you excuse me," I said, reaching for the door. "I have to go."

I had to find Marcus. He would know what to do. At least, I prayed he would.

Father Marcus was my mentor and my boss at St. John's. He was an older man at sixty five, but that did not damper his zest for life. Marcus was quite invested in the local community. He officiated at all the weddings, oversaw the bake sales, and everyone came to him first if they had a problem. He was a priest's priest. The kind of man I hoped I would be when I was older.

I found him taking a call in his office. I entered quietly and stood nearby not wanting to disturb him. Whoever was on the other side of the line was doing most of the talking. Marcus' expression said it all; it was not good news.

"Yes, I understand," he said. "Thank you."

He replaced the receiver in its cradle and looked up.

"Eric," he said. "I didn't hear you come in."

"I didn't want to interrupt," I replied. "Who was on the phone?"

"Our contact in Rome," he said.

"So it's true then," I said, deflated.

"You've heard? How?" he asked.

"A woman in confession told me. She thought I already knew."

"I'm sorry Eric," he said. "You should've heard it from me."

"What does Rome want us to do?" I asked.

"Our job; we're to help the people."

"You do realize there's going to be a lot people frightened over something that may be just another hoax."

"The church is taking it seriously. That's all that matters," he replied.

"This can't be true," I pleaded.

"I hope not," he said, "but we have to prepare for the worst."

It's hard to rest when you know exactly when you're going to die. Since sleep was not in the cards, I spent my time in the study trying to write the morning mass. People were going to be looking for reassurance and I had to find it.

I didn't know what to say to them. I believed God to be merciful and benevolent. He would never allow this to happen to his children, but this went beyond mere divinity. There were other forces at work, factors that I had no control over. I stared down at the page praying to find the words.

Five minutes to ten, Marcus and I looked into the main room to see how many people were attending. We expected a full house. We had much more than that. Every pew was full. There was not a single spot of carpet that didn't have a person sitting or standing. The head count was well above what the fire marshal would allow, but I doubted the people here would care. They were lost and were looking to us.

"Will you look at that?" Marcus said.

"Have we ever had a crowd like that?" I asked.

"Never," he said.

Marcus waved some papers in my face. I recognized my handwriting.

"This is good," he said.

"Just something I was working on," I replied.

"I want you to use it today," he said.

My jaw dropped for several reasons. One, I rarely spoke at the pulpit. I had only

done so a handful of times, usually when
Marcus was sick. Secondly, that was not the
speech I prepared for him. It was something I
scribbled out to make sense of the madness.
Now he wanted me to read it to our
congregation. I didn't know whether to be
flattered or concerned for his judgment.

"You're serious?" I asked.

Marcus nodded. "Go. Speak to them."

Good morning,

*Thank you for coming. All of us have
been told of this unthinkable development. That
everything in this world shall cease to be in
three days time. The hour of the end is
unknown. I know that isn't what you came to
hear from me. However, we should not concern
ourselves with that right now. We have been
given a priceless opportunity in the next three
days. We can shape our world for the better.*

*After this, I want you to go home and
live. Use this time God has given you. Be with
the ones you love. Hold your children close.
Laugh and reminisce. That is all I can say. If
these turn out to be our final moments, then at
least we should have the courage to live like we
never could before. If we find ourselves to be
okay in three days time, we shall know it to be
a second chance, one we did not squander.*

*I have hope. Hope for the future. That
tomorrow will come. I have it in spite of the
darkness I've seen in some; for I have also
seen glorious light. The goodness man springs
forth from himself. It gives me pause and
makes my case that we are worth saving.*

Know that God watches over you, loving you as his children. No matter what happens, we shall be taken in his loving grace and he shall bless us with eternal life.

In the name of the Father, the Son, and of the Holy Spirit. Amen.

Let us pray.

I thought of Mom and Dad. I was glad they weren't around for this. They died nine years ago, killed by a drunk driver on their way home. It was mercifully quick for them. They didn't feel a thing. The other driver survived and was rewarded with a twenty year sentence. I was a sophomore in college then. People expected me to forgive him, but I couldn't for a very long time. The man had taken my family away. He had left me alone.

It amazes me it took this long to ponder the real reasons I joined the seminary. If anyone had asked me I would've given them a stock answer about having a deep relationship with God. The reality was more complex. While my faith in God is true, it becomes clear to me that my heart wasn't fully into it. I know that the vow I took wasn't something to be thought of lightly. Yet, it is obvious that I was running from the very beginning, even though it was subconsciously. Running away from my problems, the pain I felt, and her.

Afterwards, most of our congregation left. I hoped what I said made some impact. People wasted enough time already. I didn't want them to waste anymore. A few stayed behind to pray. Marcus and I left them in silence.

Having a few moments to ourselves, I retreated back to Marcus' office. He was sitting at his desk, his head in his hands. A bottle of scotch sat nearby along with a chilled glass. He had been drinking. Normally I would be concerned, but if anyone needed a drink right now it was us.

"Hitting the bottle eh?" I asked low key.

Marcus looked up and shrugged weakly.

"Not much else to do now," he said. "What can I say?"

"How about 'would you like a glass?'"

"Would you like a glass?"

"You bet I do," I said.

Marcus pulled out one and clinked in a few ice cubes. He poured a generous swath of liquor over them and I sipped it slowly.

"This is exquisite," I said.

"Better be. Sixteen year old Scotch; been saving it for a special occasion," he said.

I nodded. "What did you think?" I asked.

"I think you did well," he said.

"Thanks padre," I replied.

"No problem."

When I returned to the main hall, everyone had left except one young lady. She was a girl really, fifteen or so. She was dressed rather demurely, a simple white summer dress and her blond hair was tied back in a ponytail. Her eyes were shut tight and she whispering a prayer. I know I should've left well enough alone, but something compelled me to walk over and speak to her.

"Are you all right, my child?" I asked.

Her eyes snapped open. "Yes, Father."

"There's no need to be formal," I said. "The service is over. You can call me Eric if that's easier for you."

"Okay," she said unsure. "I'm Lily."

"Hello Lily. Mind if I take a seat?" I asked.

"Sure," she said.

"Is there anything that troubles you?" I asked.

"Besides the obvious?" she said.

I nodded.

""It's just that everything is happening so fast. One minute we're fine, the next, total destruction. I mean I'm only fifteen, I haven't even lost my virginity—"

With that last bit of information, she cut herself off, turning red with embarrassment. That made two of us.

"I shouldn't have said that. I feel mortified," she said, wincing.

"It's okay. What you say stays between us," I replied, trying to bring normalcy back to the conversation.

"Thanks Father, I mean Eric," she said.

"What else troubles you, Lily?" I asked.

"Life," she stated simply.

"Meaning what exactly?"

"How short it is. Everyone expects to see old age. I'm not even going to see sixteen."

"We're never given enough time. Life is but a moment. You have to be grateful for what you have."

"It's just not fair," she finally said, using the old cliché trope.

"None of this is, but remember what I said. Go live. Leave no stone unturned. Perhaps God will shine on us. Make this mess go away. If not, at least you can say you lived with no regret. This isn't the best answer, but it's the only one I got."

"It's okay," she said. "It helps."

Lily headed for the door but turned back around. She still had something on her mind.

"Father?" she asked.

"Yes, Lily?"

"I need some guidance; about my other problem."

Her unintended outburst; I was trying to forget that part, but she asked.

"I'm probably not the best person to talk about this," I said.

"I don't have anyone else," she noted.

"Okay then," I said. "Ask away."

She started and stopped several times in asking a question. I was uncomfortable with the whole situation as is, but it became clear I would have to ask the first question.

"Do you have someone in mind?" I asked.

"I have this friend," she said.

"Does he have a name?"

"Ben."

"Does he like you?"

"Yes."

"And you like him?"

"Yes but—"she began.

I cut her off. "No buts. I've seen too many people defer happiness for foolish reasons. You know what you should do?"

"What?" she asked.

"Go see him tonight. Tell him how really feel. You never know, he might feel the same way; at the very least you won't have regret for not saying it."

"Okay," Lily said. "Thank you."

"Get home my child. It's late."

"One more question if I may Father? It's slightly personal, so you don't have to answer if you don't want to."

"I have nothing to hide," I said.

"Did you ever have a first love and what was her name?"

"Samantha," I said, not missing a beat. "Her name was Samantha."

I met Samantha in study hall during my junior year of high school. She was unlike any girl I had ever known before. Most girls found me to be invisible, someone they interacted with during classroom assignments, but no one that existed after that.

Samantha was different. She actually got to know me. I was this shy guy and she went out of her way to coax me out of my shell. I will always be in her debt for that. She helped me find my way. In return, I discovered what was beyond the pretty girl, the things most guys would've ignored outright.

Usually when a guy and a girl become friends, it's usually because one doesn't see the other "that way." We were somewhere in the middle. There was mutual attraction. We just chose not to act on it. We were afraid what would happen. Not with being happy together, who wouldn't want to date their best friend? No, we were concerned with consequences. If it went bad, we would lose each other, and we didn't want that.

Like everything though, something had to give. It was just after graduation. Her parents went off for the weekend so we had the place to ourselves. We were at her house sipping beers we stole from the fridge. One minute we were joking around as usual when something changed. It was as if a switch was flipped. We no longer looked at each other as friends. We began making out. I don't remember which one made the first move, but it's a minute detail. We both wanted it.

Since we didn't have to worry about being caught, I took my time. She was patient with me, coaching me in the finer arts of the act. I did my best to please her. I was always a quick learner. Later, I held her as she slept and in the darkness I realized for the first time in my life I was actually happy.

We had the summer together, but we were heading off to different schools after that. We both knew a long distance relationship was not in the cards, so we reluctantly parted ways. A few years into college and after my parents were killed, I moved towards seminary school and the path of priesthood.

I lost touch with her a few years ago. Last I heard she works for a firm in New York City. I hope she's happy. That's all I would want. At the time, I guess I thought it was best that I left her behind too. Now I wonder, should I have fought for her? Things could've been different. Maybe, we would've still been together.

St. John's runs a soup kitchen for the local community. We feed the homeless so no one has to go hungry. It was a reminder that the sacrifices I made were worth it if someone was affected for the better.

I served food with Marcus and a few of our altar boys; looking at the faces, it broke my heart. I wished I could help them all. It was of course impossible. The first thing you learn as a priest is that you can't save everyone. At most, all you can do is alleviate pain for a day, an hour, whatever it may be. That was supposed to be enough, but not for me. Now with everything happening it just became especially cruel.

Later that night I was sitting with Marcus in his office. He had been drinking again. I declined a glass. I didn't want to be numb. I wanted to feel it all. I needed to.

"Almost there, aren't we?" Marcus asked.

"I guess," I replied, noticing how drunk he was.

"Still think this is a hoax?"

"I don't know," I said. "It's got me thinking though."

"About what?" he asked.

"About my life; if this is what I really want."

"What are you talking about?"

"I think you know exactly what I'm talking about," I said, sharper than I intended.

Marcus clapped his glass down hard on the desk. It made a crack like a pistol shot. His features tightened and it was obvious that he was angry.

"Are you saying what I think you are?" he asked.

"I guess I am," I said.

"Eric, is this a game to you?"

"No."

"Sounds like it. You think you can just come into this and leave when you 'Don't feel like it?' This is supposed to be a lifelong commitment son."

"I know that, but everything going on made me realize things that I never thought about. I can't be certain anymore that I made the right decision."

"Then why did you even join—"

"I was running away Marcus!" I said exasperated. "I was twenty and had two dead parents and a broken heart. Haven't you ever done something when you weren't thinking straight? I was scared and alone so I looked to God for an answer. I thought this was it. Maybe I was wrong."

Marcus appeared as if he was about to deliver a sharp rebuttal, but he just exhaled and let his anger flow out of him.

"Figures," he said. "I knew you had some issues from the beginning."

"Marcus," I said calmly. "I don't know what to do."

"You need a sign," Marcus said.

"Pardon me?" I asked.

"When I need an answer to a hard question, I look for a sign from God. They might not seem like signs at first, but they are. You need to find yours. No matter the answer it gives, I'll support you. I owe you that much."

Marcus handed me a glass of Scotch.

"Come on," he said. "Have a drink with me."

I didn't sleep that night either. I couldn't shut my brain off, but I was unwilling to leave the warmth of my bed. I kept my eyes shut, thinking that would at least count for something. I let my mind wander. I wondered how people were coping. Would there be acceptance or panic. Would they make the most of their time or waste it frivolously as if nothing had changed. The variables ran through my mind. It kept me busy as life ticked forward to oblivion.

Saturday was a revolving door of lost souls. It got so bad that we had to pass out numbered tickets and took people in order. The subjects they wanted to talk about went through the gamut. Love, loss, children, you name it; we talked about it all. I was stressed and in great need for time to decompress. I'd never experienced this level of pressure before in my life. People were clamoring for our help in every spot you could sit or stand.

I did what I could. I didn't always have the best response, but I answered as honestly as I could. Through all this I could think of only one thing. I needed the day to be over as chilling as the thought was.

It took time and determination, but we were able to see everyone that requested an audience with us. We started early and by that point it was almost five. We would have a few hours to recuperate before the evening mass. I was about to lock up my office when there was a knock. That knock turned out to be the sign I had been searching for. I looked and found a ghost from my past.

"Hello Eric," Samantha said.

It was odd to have her standing in my doorway. She hadn't lost an ounce of her beauty. It had been refined, but the features remained the same. My heart raced. I remembered why I had loved her. Why maybe I still did.

"Samantha?" I asked, surprised.

"In the flesh, padre," she said.

"What are you doing here?"

"Family still lives here..." she said, tapering off. "If I was going to be somewhere, I might as well be with them."

"Understandable," I said.

"Look at you," she said.

"Look at me."

"If somebody told me you would be here ten years ago, I thought they'd be mad."

"That makes two of us," I said.

She laughed.

"How are you doing?" I asked.

"I'm fine," she said, pointing to a chair nearby. "Mind if I sit down?"

"Of course," I said.

She took a seat, removing her short heels, rubbing her feet.

"Thanks," she said. "Damn shoes were killing me."

"No problem," I said.

"As to your question, I've been okay. I've been working in New York, the money's good and I'm moving up the ladder or at least I was. Had a boyfriend; he decided to dump me. He was a jerk," she scoffed.

"His loss," I said, meaning it.

"What about you?" she asked.

"I'm good. I have my work," I said, leaning on my desk. "How did you know where to find me?"

"My mother still keeps tabs on you. She thought you were going to be her future son-in-law."

"I see," I said with a slight grin.

"You had to disappoint her," she said, grinning back.

"You can't please everyone. What brings you here?"

"It's been awhile. I wanted to see you."

"Same here," I said truthfully.

"I've been thinking of you a lot recently," she said her voice just above a whisper.

There could be no doubt now. The answer was right in front of me. Thinking about her was no accident. It was part of something deeper that I never confronted. I was scared to consider I had made the wrong choice.

"Thinking about me how?" I asked, not sure if I wanted to hear her answer or not.

"About us," she said.

"Samantha—"I began.

"I know how this sounds. You have so much to deal with. The last thing you need is more drama."

I didn't respond. She sighed.

"I'm sorry," she continued, "but I have to say this or I never will. I still have feelings for you."

The only woman I had ever loved sat there and said she always cared about me. It was too much to think about.

"Are you going to attend tonight?" I asked, diverting the subject.

"I might," she said.

"If you do, come find me after," I said. "We'll talk more."

"Okay," she said, turning to leave.

Marcus and I had dinner together. We ate in silence.

"You are never going to believe who walked into my office," I said, breaking it.

"Who?" Marcus asked.

So I told him. About Samantha, our personal history, how we lost track of one another. How she found me and what she had to say.

Marcus let out a low whistle. "A lot to take in eh?" he said.

"You got that right," I replied.

"What did you say?"

"I told her we'd talk later."

"How do you feel about it?" he asked.

"I'm conflicted," I said.

Marcus nodded. "You still love her?"

I shrugged. "She was the first, actually the only girl I ever loved. You never forget those."

"You're not leaving me now are you?" he asked, obviously concerned I was going to bail now at the very end.

"No," I said.

"Good," he said.

"What are your thoughts?"

Marcus sighed. "Eric, you've done good work here, but there are other ways to serve. God would understand. I would understand. We have so few chances to be happy. He'd want you to take every opportunity, if that is what you really want."

Marcus could tell I was having difficulty articulating a response. He pressed on.

"All I'm saying is," he said. "Pray that Monday comes. That way you have a choice."

Good evening,

Thank you all for coming tonight. We all know time is precious so Father Marcus and I appreciate you being here.

Faith is empowering. To carry such a strong belief in an all powerful God gives us the strength to face any challenge. I look out into the crowd and see fear and I understand the fear, but now is your test of faith. Believe in God, believe in his power and his promise of everlasting life. Regardless of what happens in the next few days this is not the end, not if you truly believe.

Some of you look to me for reassurance. You want me to lie if necessary. I don't need to lie although the truth is I don't know what is going to happen tomorrow. What I know is this; that in order to find salvation, you need to put your trust in God. Trust he will see us through this and bring us once more into the light.

In the name of the Father, the Son, and of the Holy Spirit. Amen

Let us pray.

Samantha and I sat in my office later. I wasn't able to talk to her immediately. People came up wishing to speak to me and I couldn't turn them away. Their lives had deviated from expected outcomes. How time distorts things. Samantha didn't mind. She crossed paths with an old friend and was able to catch up.

"I don't know how you do it, speak so eloquently that is," Samantha said.

"I'm just good at it, I guess," I said.

"So," she said, trying to change the subject.

"So," I replied back.

"Did you think about what I said?" she asked, keeping her voice low.

"Yes," I said.

"And?" she asked.

I froze up. I know what I wanted to say, but the words wouldn't come out.

"Sam, I—"

"Do you love me?" she asked, "Please. I just want to know. Give me that at least."

A pause.

"Yes," I said.

Samantha broke out in a combination of a laugh and a sob. I couldn't tell if she was happy or sad; probably both.

"You were the only one that cared for me," she said.

"That's not true," I said, trying to reassure her.

"Perhaps, but I've dated a lot of guys. None of them treated me like you did."

Silence.

"We should've made it work," she said finally.

I nodded.

She stood up to leave, draping her coat over her arm.

"Thanks for seeing me, Eric."

She went to leave, but I got up and met her at the doorway.

"Samantha. Wait," I said.

"Yes?" she replied.

"Do you believe in second chances?" I asked.

"I do," she said, her eyes hopeful.

"If we get ours, I'm going to take some time, figure out what I want. Perhaps, we could try again Sam, if you want to."

She smiled, a tear rolling down her face. She wiped it away.

"Okay," she said.

"Okay," I replied. "I'll see you soon."

"Not if I see you first."

"A *Stand by Me* reference? Really?"

"You have your thing, I have my mine."

"Still—"I smirked.

"Eric?"

"Yes—"

She grabbed the back of my neck and pulled me close. She pressed her lips hard against mine and held them there. In that moment I remembered the spark. What made us, us. When she finally let go, I felt dazed.

"Just in case," she said, leaving.

For the first time in two days I was finally able to rest. It was bound to happen. When you are unable to sleep for long periods of time, your body finally gives up. I couldn't be more grateful. I didn't have to think anymore. Or so I thought.

I was in a church. It wasn't St. John's. It was much bigger, with multiple floors and a dome ceiling skylight that the bright sun shined through. It was bigger than anything the Vatican had by far. My eyes darted to all corners, searching for signs of life. I found no one. I sat down at one of the pews and exhaled slowly, closing my eyes.

"Not laying down on the job are you padre?" a voice called out.

My eyes snapped open, alert. I gazed to the left of me and found Father Marcus sitting there. He held a bible and was gingerly flipping through it, page by page.

"Marcus?" I asked.

"Not exactly, my son," he said.

I didn't get the meaning.

"What are you doing here? Where am I?"

"I'm always here," he said. "This is my home."

"What do you mean?" I asked.

Marcus let silence be his answer.

I sat in disbelief.

"I take many forms my son," he said.

"This is not happening."

"And yet here we are talking to each other."

"This isn't real. This is a dream," I said.

"Of course it is," he said, shrugging as if it was obvious.

"Why are you here?" I asked.

"To talk," he said.

"Talk to me?"

"Yes my son. You have a lot on your mind. The world, the people in your church, the woman you love. You are lost my son. You're wondering if you will be able to figure it out."

I nodded. "Will I?"

"I cannot answer that," he said.

"But you're..." I hesitated saying the word. I decided not to press it. "So what do I do?" I asked. "What is the right thing?"

Marcus, or rather the entity that took his appearance, gave a puzzled expression.

"Look to yourself. You shall find it."

"What does that even mean?" I asked, getting frustrated.

"One day," he said, heading for the door. "You'll know."

I woke up at eight in the morning. Today was Sunday. Everything was supposed to end, but the outside didn't show a speck of doom and gloom. The birds chirped and the grass continued to grow. Everything looked completely normal, which I guess was the point.

I only had an hour before what possibly could be the final mass I would ever give no matter the outcome. I showered briskly and shaved the stubble from my face.

I found Marcus in the kitchen. He was cooking up a storm. I suddenly felt hungry.

"Dig in," he said. "Might as go out with a full stomach."

I couldn't have agreed more with him and began to eat.

"Marcus," I began. "I found my sign."

"The girl?" he asked, knowingly.

I nodded. "I'm going to take some time. Decide whether or not I want to stay. If I don't, maybe she and I might try again. See what happens."

"I thought as much, but you're not there yet," he said. "Get ready. Either way, this could be it for you."

Good morning,

I have always believed in the grace of God. I believe that he watches over us, all of us, the best he can. Now, our greatest test of faith is upon us. Our faith needs to be stronger now more than ever.

We need to pray for our salvation. Not just for your own, but for those you hold closest to your heart. To those who need it most. If we pray for the salvation of others, perhaps we shall too be saved. Perhaps if we are saved we can then work on making our world a much better place than before.

In the name of the Father, the Son, and of the Holy Spirit. Amen.

Let us pray.

As the congregation slowly filed out, I went around the pews and replaced the bibles into their holders. I could hear footsteps behind me and when I turned to look I saw another familiar face.

"Hello Eric," Lily said.

"Hey," I replied. "What are you doing here?"

"I came to say goodbye," she said. "And I wanted to thank you."

"Thank me for what?"

"He kissed me."

I smiled. "I'm happy for you," I said.

"I have to go," she said. "My parents don't know I'm here, but I had to see you. Take care of yourself, Eric."

"Take care, Lily," I said.

And just like that, Marcus and I were alone in the church. We sat at the pulpit, side by side, downing glasses of scotch as we waited for the end to happen, or not.

"Marcus, do you really think it's going to happen?" I asked.

Marcus shrugged his shoulders. "I don't know. Against every shred of evidence, I still have faith that we'll be okay. For faith is being sure of what we hope for and certain of what we do not see."

"Hebrews, 11:1," I replied.

"You still know your scripture."

"That I do. That will never change Marcus."

"You don't have to stay Eric," Marcus said, his voice soft with emotion. "You should be with her."

"I know," I replied. "The thing is, Marcus, you've been like a father to me, ever since mine died. I'm not going to leave you. Not now."

Marcus smiled for the first time in three days. "Thanks padre," he said.

"No problem."

"Eric?"

"Yes?"

"Will you pray with me?"

"Of course I will," I said.

We knelt to our knees and begun to pray. I don't know what Marcus thought of as he prayed. As for me, I prayed for my congregation, for Lily, for Samantha. I recited my prayers as fast as my lips could carry them.

God would hear them.

He had to.

ANNA

I never thought I would be a mother. I didn't plan on having children at all. I was never that type of girl. Normal maternal instincts didn't seem to apply to me. I didn't hate children. On the contrary, I had plenty friends that had kids and they were the cutest things. However, that longing was never a part of me though. That was before I met Nick.

Nick is the kind of guy you can bring home to Mom. He didn't know much about my reluctance for motherhood and he had made no overtures concerning fatherhood so it was a non-issue. We were nowhere near marriage as is. Things were good and I wasn't going to ruin it by rocking the boat. Eventually my hand was forced by fate.

Long story short, I got pregnant. My first instinct was to get rid of it. I was young, and still had many things I wanted to do sans the responsibility of a child. I know how that makes me sound, but nine months is a long time to be carrying another person around. You'd think evolution would've streamlined the process by now. Despite my feelings on the issue, I had to tell Nick. Perhaps he would feel the same way about us not being ready and it wouldn't be a big deal.

His reaction was not what I expected. Most guys would have gone pale if their gal had uttered those two particular words. Not Nick, he grinned and picked me off the floor, twirling me around. He was so happy about becoming a father. I kept my doubts to myself.

I didn't know how he would react to them. Besides, I loved him, maybe this was for the best.

I had met Nick at a coffee shop open mike night. One of those poetry readings where nervous people read their stuff praying they don't get booed off stage. My girlfriends had dragged me out there that night. I thought of dozens of excuses to get out of it, but none were remotely plausible. As it was, I owed Teri, my best friend a favor so there I was, drinking bad coffee that singed the roof of my mouth as I watched a parade of awful poets exit the stage.

Nick was the last to perform. He didn't look like much at first glance. He was in dire need of a haircut for one and his sense of fashion wasn't anything to write home about. In my mind these would usually be deal breakers, but on this night, it came across as quaint, quirky. It illustrated to me that he wasn't phony. His poetry wasn't half bad either.

Unlike the others, he at least had the audience's attention. They held onto what he said. He had a knack for it. What I noticed the most were not the words he used, but how he said them. His poetry had a sad feel to it. His delivery was soulful, with a touch of mourning. It was like it was painful for him to say it aloud. Maybe it was. When he was finished, there was an eerie silence. Then audience began to clap. Only this time they meant it.

"I want him," Teri said.

I forgot to mention. My friend Teri is a whore. She went after any guy that wasn't nailed down. Sometimes, she took those too. I once asked her why she acted that way. She told me that she loved the hunt. Guys did it all the time, she said. Why couldn't she do the same? I couldn't find fault in her reasoning.

"Of course you do," I shot back, shaking my head in disbelief. "You want every guy."

"At least I admit it," she said.

That was true. If anything, Teri was brutally honest about who she is. I had a problem with that. The truth was I wanted to go talk to Nick myself. I felt something when he spoke. He was worth giving a shot. That wouldn't happen if Teri got to him first. He'd be persona non grata after that. I decided to leave it to chance.

"I'll play you for him," I said.

Teri looked surprised. I'd never challenged her for a guy before, but there was a first time for everything.

"What?" she asked.

"Rock, paper, scissors," I said. "You game?"

"You know I never lose."

"Then you have nothing to worry about. I'll take that as a yes."

"Fine," she said.

"Okay," I said. "One, two, three, shoot."

It's funny how things work out.

I gave him my number that night. I had never done that before, but he was different. I felt the need to pursue him and make the first move. I was glad I did.

Nick was more than a coffee shop poet. He liked writing and performing, but he knew it wouldn't pay the bills. He worked at a publishing company for that. It was fitting, seeing he had an affinity for words. He spent his days searching through piles of manuscripts looking for the next great voice. His fulfillment came from molding the world with the written word. He wished that he could have the same opportunities with his poetry.

He had been published a few times in magazines, but he was a realist about it. The market was small and competitive and there was no real money in it. I asked him once why he didn't try to transition to fiction writing. He had the creativity for it. I appreciated his response:

"Poetry is much more difficult than literature," he said. "We can write something as long as we want it to be, but we're still using substantially less words than a novelist. We have to be careful with the words. We have to make them count, make them matter."

The people in my life found it odd when we started our relationship. I was never a girl who was into long term relationships. They never appealed to me. Being around boys in my teenage years turned me off to most men. I started to believe they were all the same.

Nick was different. He was a bit of a hippie, but he had his head on straight. He had a good job which most guys I had previously dated lacked. He also had interests that had nothing to do with "wrestling" or "football" and for that I was grateful.

Teri was envious of me for once. My relationship with Nick made her re-evaluate her relationship with other men. She stopped sleeping around to my surprise. For once she wanted more. She found a great guy in Michael, a guy she met at work. I was happy for her change of tune. It was exhausting to be the friend of a man eater and at least she wouldn't be trying to steal my man.

Camille, my mother, was ecstatic for me having a boyfriend. She thought it was the precursor for marriage and grandchildren. When I told her I was expecting, I swore she almost did back flips down the hallway. She called everyone. If she had the means, she would've thrown a parade.

Life was good. I had a man I loved, great friends, and a baby on the way. But life has a way of smacking you in the face when you least expect it. I had been shown good fortune and the universe felt the need to balance the scale for me and everyone I knew.

Thursday started out innocently enough. No one knew it yet, but everything was about to change. Nick had just gotten home and I was cooking dinner. It was just a simple stir fry, one of the few things I knew how to make. Either way, Nick would eat it because he had an iron stomach.

After dinner and washing dishes, Nick and I sat on the couch and watched television.

He rubbed my aching feet (which he was very good at) and I was reminded once again why I had it made. Unfortunately, there wasn't anything on. The networks were in the middle of sweeps, so programming was in reruns. It figured.

"All these channels and there's nothing on," I sighed.

"That's television for you, babe," Nick said. "Keep flipping, there's got to be something."

I went through the channels, settling on a Jane Austen movie, Mansfield Park. The one book of hers I could never finish. I liked the movie better anyway. We were near the end of the movie when Fanny was about to kiss Edmund, her true love, when the screen flickered. I thought nothing of it. Then the screen went black.

"What the hell?" I said.

"I don't know," Nick said.

"Did the power go out?"

"Don't think so."

The picture returned, but it wasn't what I expected to see. Instead, there was a bright white screen. Letters began to type out until two sentences were formed. The message was to the point.

The world was going to end in three days.

Needless to say I didn't take that well.

"This is a joke right?" I said. "Change the channel Nick."

"That's the thing, Anna," Nick said, his face going white. "I've been doing that. It's the same thing on every one."

Like many, we looked to the news for answers. We didn't get one. Just a bunch of talking heads going back and forth. Then the President came on and addressed the nation, telling us not to panic. Good luck with that. Their evasiveness meant only one thing.

"What do we do, Nick?" I asked, scared.

"What do you mean?" he asked, answering my question with another question.

"Is this real?"

"It has to be a hoax."

"What if it's not?" I said.

"Listen to me," he said, wrapping his arms around me. "Everything is going to be okay."

"You promise?"

"I promise," he said.

I wanted to believe him.

We didn't get to bed till two in the morning. Nick went out like a light. I wasn't so lucky. My usual uncomfortable position was not the problem right now. I couldn't sleep because I was thinking of the implications involving our baby.

I was only seven months pregnant. I still had eight more weeks until I delivered. That meant that if this was happening, I would never hold my child. That horrified me to no end.

We were having a girl. I imagined her sometimes all grown up. I wondered what features she would inherit from us. She would get my curly blond hair and Nick's pale blue eyes. I'd piece together parts of us into the ideal vision of what our daughter would look like.

I was happy to have a girl. Having a daughter is special. As a mother, you hope to raise her well. Give her your best qualities. Make her learn from your mistakes. I wanted that for her. Now she may not have any of it.

I woke up to the smell of bacon creeping down the hallway. Nick was apparently cooking breakfast. I walked into the kitchen to find Nick preparing more food that we could eat even if we were dying of starvation. I knew what was going on. This was his way of coping. He was pretending nothing was wrong and everything was still normal. I decided to let him have his denial for now. He might have to wake up to it eventually.

"Good morning, sweetie," he said, giving me a quick peck. "Take a seat, and have what you crave."

"And if I crave everything?" I joked.

"I have plenty."

I concentrated on the food. It was delicious. My daughter seemed to approve. She was kicking lightly.

"The baby's kicking," I said.

Nick grinned. "The little rascal, she wants out. Not yet little one."

"I wish she was, because then I could hold her. I'd give anything to hold her."

Nick's grin faded. He grabbed for my hand and held it tight.

"Anna, we're going to be fine," he said.

"Okay," I replied perhaps too quickly to be convincing.

We stopped talking and focused on eating. Our utensils scraping against the plates was the only sound that could be heard outside the air conditioning coming to life.

"What would you like to do today?" he finally asked.

"Me?" I asked.

"Yes you."

"I don't know."

"There's has to be something. It's Friday, we have the whole day to ourselves."

I was about to reply with some pointless errand for us to partake in when somewhere in my mind snapped into place with a clarity I hadn't felt in a long time. He was right. There was something I wanted to do.

"I want to visit my mother," I said.

"Your mom?" he asked, concerned. "You do remember what happened last time we were there right?"

"I know, but that's what I want to do."

Mom and I have a complicated relationship which I understand is a total cliché statement, but it is the truth. When I was growing up, she acted more like my best friend than a parent, which in theory sounds great. A parent who will buy you booze and gives you condoms so you could sleep with your boyfriend. But no one was being an adult. She was currying my favor and I was having bad behavior reinforced. It took me years to realize how poisonous it was. I wasn't going to be like that with my kid.

Her reaction to my pregnancy seemed normal enough, but I knew better. Being a grandmother meant she could mold my daughter like she did me. I think it is somewhat pathological with her. Through her family, she was able to feel young again.

It should come as no surprise that we eventually had words. I made it clear to her she would have to make some changes is she wanted to be in her grandchild's life. She took it as a personal attack and came across as self absorbed. I just wanted my child to have a clean slate.

In the end though, I tried not to dwell on it. After a certain point, people don't change. We are who we are. Others either embrace it or get the hell out of your way. It's as simple as that.

It had been about a month since that altercation. We have both acted petty and I knew it. I knew I had to fix it before my daughter was born. Now with the added pressure of the latest developments, I wanted to clear the air. Make my peace, or at least try to.

It was tense from the beginning.

I had called ahead to see if was okay to stop by. She seemed shocked that I even wanted to see her, but she said it was fine. When we stepped inside her home, the place was immaculately clean. It seemed that Nick wasn't the only one trying to keep their mind off things.

Nick had always been cordial with Mom. Like most future son-in-laws, he respected her because that was what he was supposed to do. He minded his manners and helped her around her house when she needed it. Nick was nervous to be there. He was afraid of what my mother would say this time. If it was bad, he would be in the middle of it, the unwilling spectator or possibly a referee.

"So," Mom began, "How are you dear?"

"I'm fine," I said. "You?"

"The same."

"I assume you saw the message last night."

"Yes I did. Such panic over nothing," she said, her face scrunching up in displeasure.

"I hope so."

"Know so dear."

Nick excused himself to the restroom. I'm sure he knew why I had wanted to come and wanted no part of it. I wanted privacy anyways, so it was win-win.

"Why did you come here?" Mom asked her tone harsh.

"Let's not fight," I pleaded.

"You made it clear you didn't want to see me."

"That's not true."

"Is it?" she asked her voice defensive, "I don't want you poisoning my daughter you said. I don't need you messing with her head you said."

"That's right," I said. "I don't. I just need you to be a grandmother, a normal one."

"So I'm to blame for being unconventional—"

"Mom, this isn't about you! This isn't about me either."

The anger in her face deflated.

"What if what they say is true?" I asked my voice breaking.

"Anna, dear—"

"What if I never hold my little girl in my arms?"

I couldn't be in denial anymore. I broke down, and let it all out. My mother's eyes softened. She hugged me tightly. My body convulsed uncontrollably and she held on every step of the way. All I had desired was for us to reconcile, for her to be my mom again. In the quiet, we found room for each other once more.

On the drive back it started to rain. It hit the windshield softly and was quite soothing. It was a small sign that the world was still on track, for the moment at least.

"Did you find what you were looking for?" Nick asked.

Nothing got by that one.

"Yes," I replied.

"Good."

"Are we going anywhere else?"

"No," he said. "Do you need to go anywhere?"

"No," I said. "Let's go home."

Teri and Michael were coming over for dinner. The dinner we had planned for two weeks. Part of me wanted to hide away.

However, I knew seeing them would do me good and take my mind off things.

When they arrived, Nick poured them each a glass of merlot. I missed liquor so much. My world was literally crashing down, and I couldn't drink. The things I do for love.

Nick pulled another masterpiece out of thin air, creating a decadent meal that would make Gordon Ramsay weep with joy. It hit my taste buds in all the right places. If I was to have a last meal, it would probably taste something like that.

We spent dinner commiserating about old times. Teri related the story about Nick and me meeting coming down to a game of rock, paper, scissors. It got Michael every time, for he was a big believer in fate.

The day was damn near perfect. I made peace with mom, and was spending the night with my best friend and the man I loved. If this was a normal day, I would consider myself blessed. The problem was there wasn't anything normal about this day; the nagging issue was if there would even be a future.

After dinner, Nick and Michael went off to drink beers and talk about whatever guys talk about. That left Teri and me at the table. Teri was polishing off the merlot and I watched as every drop slid down her throat.

"I miss booze," I said.

"You think?" Teri said smirking. "You've been staring at me all night."

"I miss drinking. Have a baby then you'll see how it is."

"Yeah, I don't think that is going to happen," she said. Teri got a weird look on her face, realizing immediately she said something wrong.

"Sorry. I didn't mean it like that," she said.

"Don't sweat it," I said.

"How are you holding up?"

"As well as I can be."

"And Nick?"

"I think he's in denial."

"That's not good." She said.

"So you think it's going to happen too?" I asked.

Teri nodded. "Yes."

"Why?" I asked

"No one has stood up with proof showing us it's not going to happen. Not one scientist, not one intellectual has said we are overreacting, that our conclusions are foolish. So that leaves two options. They're either holding back information from the public, or there is nothing to discredit, it's real."

As a woman, it is difficult to change our minds. Once it is made up it is usually set in stone. All I could think was that I was a dead woman walking. Even as this thought crossed through my mind, I tried to dissuade myself from it. I needed to be strong for Nick and the baby.

I couldn't deny though that I was facing death. That was a bitter pill to swallow. I wasn't young per se at twenty-nine, but there was still much I wanted to do. Most of us live our lives thinking we'll live forever. I felt the same way though it was hard to be selfish when I thought of my daughter. She wasn't going to see her first birthday, let alone her first day.

I didn't sleep again. Nick was out like a light. Michael Myers could stab me to death ten feet away and he wouldn't hear a lick of the struggle. I envied him for that. If there was any time I wanted to sleep it was now.

As I laid there awake, a startling thought sent a chill up my spine. I thought my situation was unique. I was wrong. There were women all over the world that were experiencing the same thing I was. They were also thinking of the lives that weren't going to be. I felt angry. Why was this happening? Everyone wants to know the "why." Maybe there wasn't one.

Saturday morning Nick told me he was going to see his parents and his brother. I had no objections to his plans; I wanted some time to myself as is. I just needed to figure out what to do with it. I didn't want to stay cooped up in the house. I was unable to spend time with Teri since she wanted to be alone with Michael. As for Mom, I would visit her later in the day. My options limited, I decided to visit the local park.

The place is quite nice and the kids enjoy it well enough. Nick and I played tennis there and he played pickup basketball games there as well. It's a quiet spot, a place where one can play, exercise, or think without being bothered. I just wanted some fresh air.

139

I headed there around mid day. The sky was clear and it was mercifully warm. The park wasn't crowded so I had my choice of park benches. I chose to sit near the jungle gym where a handful of kids were playing on them. I watched in silence and I took in their every move. I imagined my daughter playing with them. It was too much to think about. My lip quivered. I felt so helpless. All I wanted was to be a good mother. Protect my child from harm. I couldn't stop this, no one could.

"Are you all right?" A woman's voice spoke to me.

I looked up. There was an older woman standing there.

"No," I said. "I'm not."

The woman took a seat next to me. She gingerly handed me a tissue and I took it wiping my eyes.

"You're thinking about your child aren't you?" She asked.

"How did you know?" I asked.

"Common sense, really. You're a pregnant woman watching a bunch of kids. There's probably not much else on your mind right now."

I laughed somberly. "True. Who are you with?"

"I'm with my daughter and grandson," she said. She pointed her finger to the jungle gym. "He's the boy on the slide."

"Cute."

"I'd like to think so," she said. "He eats too much sugar though; makes him hyperactive."

We watched as the kids played. They had not a care in the world. I wondered if they knew what was happening. Probably not and it was better that way. They wouldn't have been able to comprehend it anyway. Death is foreign idea to a child. You think you'll live forever. That's what I thought when I was a kid. Of course, now I knew better.

The drive to Mom's was uneventful. I expected more people on the road, but I guessed they stayed home with life crumbling around them.

I knocked on the door and waited. Mom opened up the door and smiled when she saw it was me. We were okay again.

"Come on in, sweetie," she said.

I noticed a subtle change in the air. The tenseness was absent.

"What have you been up to?" I asked.

"Not much," she replied, "mostly cleaning and looking at old photographs. I was about to make some tea. Would you like some?"

"Sure," I said.

Mom went into the kitchen to prepare the tea while I waited in the den. She had been cleaning for sure. I could smell the lemon furniture polish that saturated the air and I almost got sick. Mom returned with two mugs and handed me one. The tea was piping hot and I nearly scalded my tongue.

"Thanks, Mom," I said.

"No problem dear," she said.

"There's something I've wanted to ask you."

"Anything you want, sweetie."

"What was the best thing about being my mom?" I asked. Mom was taken aback.

"You sure you want to talk about this considering..." she trailed off.

I waved my hand in dismissal. "I want to know."

"Well then," she began, collecting her thoughts, "The best part was you had my best qualities. Despite my...numerous mistakes, you moved past them and grew up to be a beautiful, intelligent woman. A daughter I could be proud of."

"And what was the worst thing?" I asked.

"The worst thing..." she said, trailing off again.

"Mom?" I asked concerned for a moment.

"The worst part was the day I realized I couldn't always protect you," she said. "For all my efforts you still could be taken from me. My life wouldn't have much meaning after that."

The night came and went. Nick cooked and washed the dishes after while I went to lie down and watch television. My back ached and I was tired so I didn't feel like doing much else.

The news said the same things. Half were denials, half were doom and gloom. There was no middle ground. You either believed or you didn't. There seemed to be no end to the coverage. I shook my head in disgust and looked for something else to watch. There was nothing, but the news. I got frustrated, wasn't there a single chick flick on?

A loud bang knocked me out of my thoughts. It was coming from our bedroom. I shut the TV off and walked down the hallway to see what Nick was doing. I pushed the door open and peered inside. What I found pissed me off. It shouldn't have, but that was the emotion at hand.

Nick was putting together the baby's crib. He had parts strewn all over the floor and a large unfolded set of directions on the bed along with his tool belt. He reached for a socket wrench and attached two pieces together. He had no clue I was behind him.

"What the hell are you doing?" I blurted out.

Nick jumped a little on the floor.

"Jesus, babe, you scared me," he said.

"I asked what you are doing."

"I'm putting together the crib," he said as he continued to work. "We'll need it soon enough."

"No, we won't," I said unable to mask my bitterness.

"Of course we will honey," he replied.

"Just stop it Nick."

"Stop what?"

"Stop pretending everything is okay! Have you seen the fucking news? The world is ending. Everyone dies. You, me, the—"I was going to say "baby", but I couldn't push the word out of my mouth.

"Calm down Anna," he said.

"Calm? All you are is calm. I get what you're doing; you're trying to be the supportive boyfriend. You know what I want? I want you to be mad. This is happening. This is serious. Stop pretending."

"I'm not pretending," he said.

"You're putting together a crib that won't be used because our daughter won't even be born," I snapped, instantly regretting it.

Nick looked at me like I had never seen him do before. For a moment I thought he might hit me, but that wasn't in his nature. He just stood there real quiet and excruciatingly calm.

"Do you think I'm blind Anna?" he finally asked.

"The way you've been acting, yes," I replied.

"I'm not."

"Then what is going on?"

"I've been trying to keep you calm!" he screamed.

I didn't know how to respond to that, but it didn't matter. He just barreled on with what he had to say.

"Ever since that message showed up, I've been trying to keep positive, for you! So you wouldn't lose hope. I've been trying to protect you. That's what a man does. He protects his family."

A flood of emotions crashed over me. I had been so wrong about him.

"Oh, Nick—"I said.

"What good is a man if he can't protect his family?" he asked.

With that, his final bit of armor fell. He came to me and held me tight. I knew then that I loved him more in that moment than the first night we had met. His body felt frail in my arms as he held on to me.

"Shh, it's okay," I said, now the one doing the comforting, "We're going to be all right, remember? It's just you and me, you and me against the world."

I called the only person who would listen without judgment; Teri. I dialed her number praying she would pick up. Luckily, she did.

"Hey," she said.

"Hi," I said.

"What's wrong?"

"Outside the obvious?"

"Obviously."

"I had a big fight with Nick," I said.

"Start from the beginning," she replied. "I'll need to know everything."

I gave her the speed version of what happened. Teri stayed silent.

"You have a great guy," she finally said. "I'm glad you won that night."

"Really?" I asked.

"Yes. I would've ruined him anyway."

We laughed.

"Thanks," I said.

"No problem," she said, "Anna?"

"Yeah?"

"Everything is going to be fine."

I felt choked up, on the verge of tears.

"Okay," I said.

"Take care of yourself," she said.

"You too," I said.

"And Anna?"

"Yes?"

"Love you," she said.

"Love you too," I said.

"Sunday morning rain is falling, steal some covers, share some skin..."

Song lyrics crossed through my head as I woke up Sunday morning. It was quiet. I tried not to think about it. I was comfy next to the man I loved. I snuggled closer to him and kissed him softly. His eyes fluttered awake.

"Morning," I said.

"Morning," he said.

"I'm sorry about last night."

"It's okay."

"No it's not," I said.

"I don't blame you," he replied.

I sighed softly and rubbed my stomach. My little girl was still asleep. "What's going to happen to us?"

"Give me your hand," he said.

I reached over and he interlocked his fingers with mine.

"No matter what happens," Nick said. "We're going to stay together, as a family."

"You promise?" I asked.

"I promise," he said.

JOSHUA

There's nothing fair about who lives and who dies.

That is the first lesson you learn as a doctor. It doesn't sink in until you lose your first patient. You give it your all and it still isn't enough. It's a harsh lesson, but you need to remember sometimes it's not up to you. There are other forces at work.

I've been a doctor for over twelve years. It doesn't get any easier for me to lose a patient. I've saved countless lives. I only count the ones I've lost. You do not want to know that number. It keeps me awake at night.

When I first entered college I was unsure on what route I wanted to take. Becoming a doctor slowly became the clearest choice. I wanted to do something that mattered. I wanted to help people. Between school and my residency, it seemed like forever. I left with a large amount of debt, but I made it through with my license. I consider that one of the proudest days of my life.

Being a doctor requires several things. It requires empathy and at the same time emotional distance from your patients. You have to have a stomach made of iron; the human body is full of unpleasantness. Medicine requires courage; it may not be "run into a burning building" courage, but it is courage all the same. You need tenacity, to face the trenches day after day. Being a doctor means you will make great sacrifices. I was about to learn the hard way.

I was coming off a long shift at the hospital on Thursday afternoon. I was running on fumes and looking forward to spending time with my wife and kids. Angela is nine and Tyler is seven. They're hyper, but who isn't at that age. They are my entire world.

The same can be said of my wife, Marie. We've been married for fifteen years now. I met her during my residency via a mutual friend. The moment I saw her, I knew I would marry her. Our marriage has remained strong despite the stress my job brings. To anyone considering tying the knot, remember that marriage is a lot of work. If you are not ready for that, don't start. It will only end with someone getting hurt.

I pulled into the driveway and rubbed my tired eyes. I could see the lawn needed to be mowed. I would have to take care of that before my next shift. I chuckled at the thought of a day in the near future when I could make Tyler do it; one less chore I'd have to worry about.

When my key hit the door, Marie was already there. She looked frazzled, but her beauty still shined through. To me, she is still radiant as the first night I saw her.

"Hi honey," I said, closing the door.

Her expression said it all.

"The kids?" I asked.

"They are off the wall," she said. "I made sure that they didn't have any sugar too."

I kissed her on the cheek. "Give me a sec, I'll handle them," I said.

I placed my bag down in the closet and hung up my coat. I could hear Angela and Tyler in the living room watching cartoons, the television seemingly at full volume. I walked in there and noticed outside of the noise of the TV, they were behaving themselves considering. They sat on the couch, watching the screen intently.

"Hi monkeys," I said.

"Daddy!" Angela shrieked.

"Hi Dad," Tyler said.

"You are giving your mother grief," I said with a tinge of humor.

"Not on purpose," Angela said defensively.

"We've been bored today," Tyler replied.

"You want to do me a huge favor?" I asked.

"Sure," They said in unison.

"Go up to your room and play quietly," I said, giving them a grin to show I wasn't mad. "Give your poor mother a break okay?"

"Okay," Angela said, shutting off the TV.

They jumped off the couch and scampered upstairs. They sure could be a handful. I haven't been around much lately so most of the parenting had been relegated to Marie. I needed to be home more often. I made a mental note to talk to HR about getting some time off.

Marie peeked into the room and exhaled in gratitude.

"Thank you," She said. "They were driving me nuts."

"No problem," I said. "I do what I can."

"You do huh?"
"Yes."

As a favor to me for handling the kids, Marie let me rest for a few minutes uninterrupted before we cooked dinner. We made fried chicken; it was nice to eat something that didn't come out of a vending machine. The kids liked it as always, their faces comically speckled with food. Marie tried in vain to keep them clean, but they would just get messy again with the next bite.

After dinner was over, and the kids were off doing God knows what, I cleaned up the mess and loaded the dishwasher. With that done, I plopped myself on the couch and began to flip the channels. I just wanted to relax. Marie joined me after awhile and we snuggled together, her head resting on my shoulder. It was nice to have her close. There was nothing on so we compromised and watched *The Princess Bride*. I had yet to see it all the way through. Marie swore she'd make me get through it this time.

"So how was work?" she asked.

"It was okay," I said.

"Nothing bad happen?"

"Define 'bad'."

"You know what I mean."

"No," I said. "I didn't lose anyone."

"Good," she said. "You shouldn't beat yourself up though. It's not good for you."

"Keeps me sharp," I replied.

Marie didn't respond, just nuzzled closer.

We returned our attentions to the movie and for full hour let it take us in. We were near the ending, the part I had always missed. I was going to get through it this time. Or at least I would have, if it wasn't for the blackout.

The entire screen went black. At first I thought the power had gone out but dismissed it since we still had electricity everywhere else. Perhaps a cord had gone bad.

"What was that?" Marie asked.

"I don't know," I said. "Let me check the wiring."

I got off the couch and begun to look behind the console and inspect the wires. Nothing seemed out of place. Nothing was frayed. Everything was normal.

"Josh," Marie said.

"Everything seems to be fine," I replied.

"No, Josh. Look," she said.

I looked back to the screen. It was a bright white. Letters began to form and they formed two sentences that changed everything.

The end of the world, that's what the message promised. In three days everything would be gone. It was unthinkable. It had to be a prank, a teenage hacker maybe. I flipped through all the channels. They all had the same message. I started to get spooked.

"Josh," Marie said. "What the hell is going on?"

"I wish I knew," I said.

The screen turned back to normal. The programs were on like nothing had happened. It didn't take long for the twenty four hour news channels to start their coverage. They knew as little as we did. The authorities were "investigating". The President even came on in an emergency press conference and told the nation not to panic.

Yeah. Good luck with that.

Marie put the kids to bed early. She justified it by saying they were going to do some fun stuff tomorrow. There is nothing like good old fashioned bribery to keep children in step. They were asleep soon enough.

Marie and I were a different matter. The best course of action would be to try and get some sleep. We could figure things out in the morning. It would be difficult to rest with this looming over our heads, though. I wound up getting less than four. The phone rang on the dresser and I grabbed it.

"Yeah," I said into the receiver.

"Josh? It's Adam."

Adam was a friend and colleague; we went to medical school together and worked together since his transfer from Pittsburgh. Adam was a good doctor, a dependable guy.

"What's up?" I asked. "You do realize what hour it is right?"

"You've heard?" he asked back.

"Yes."

"I'll cut to the chase, Josh. The hospital is swamped. I hate to ask this, but I need you to come in. We need everyone on deck right now. Just for twelve hours, please."

I sighed, but this had happened before.

"Okay," I said, pulling myself out of bed. "I'll be there in twenty minutes or so."

The water felt nice against my skin. I kept my head under the nozzle for a long time trying to use the heat to will myself awake. It was not helping. I needed to sleep, but it was not in the cards today nor possibly for the rest of my days.

I felt a hand on my shoulder and I was startled. Marie stood there naked. She closed the door.

"Hey," I said. "Sorry I woke you."

"It's okay," she said. "I thought I'd join you."

"I see."

"When do you have to be there?"

"I told Adam twenty minutes."

"Think you could stretch that a little?" she asked, her voice coy.

"I think I can," I said.

Adam wasn't kidding. The place was like a warzone. When I walked in, the sound was unbearable. Nurses and orderlies were scrambling with charts and medicine. Everyone was moving at a fast clip. I'd have never seen anything like it before.

"Josh," Adam called out. "Thank god you came."

"No problem," I replied. "Sorry about the delay. Traffic was bad."

"No big deal," he said. "You came and that's all that matters. I need you on the third floor. It's a fucking mess. They're killing each other out there. Apparently, the end of the world started a bit early."

"I'll get right up there," I said.

It wasn't until hours later that I was able to get a moment to take a break. Adam wasn't bullshitting. I couldn't fathom what was going through people's heads that would make them hurt each other like that.

Eight of the people I treated died. Three remained stable and another was on his way out. It is only a matter of time. It was a crappy way to start the morning. All I wanted today was to spend time with my kids and mow the lawn. Now I may never see home again. My reality had shifted, twisting into something I no longer recognized.

I shut my eyes and let the dark envelop me. I felt calm, which is ironic considering my surroundings. It could last only a moment. The intercom shrilled to life and broke it.

"Code Blue in Room 304. I repeat Code Blue in Room 304. Doctor needed stat."

I raced out the door.

The guy was already gone by the time I got there. It was quick. Rather painless for him. He was lucky really. He wouldn't have to see the world crumble. That was the burden for the rest of us. I wonder if people considered killing themselves. Thinking it was better to die now than die in the cataclysm. I didn't know. It wasn't important to the task at hand. It just made me think. I sighed to no one; it was going to be a long night. I left the room and continued my rounds.

The next few hours went by in a blur. Patients continued to flow in. They sprung up like weeds. We'd take care of one, and two more would require help. It was frustrating to say the least. In the end though, we all dug deep and did what we had to. I'd be going home soon. Spend the rest of my time with my family. Someone else would take the reins.

I was in for a rude awakening.

"I'm so sorry Josh."

That was Adam in the cafeteria. He was telling me that I couldn't leave.

"What the hell are you talking about?" I said in hushed tones, but my voice was rising.

"We are stretched thin. We don't have enough staff to run the hospital. Not even close." he said. "People are scared Josh. Can you blame them? I'm scared too. They're more concerned about themselves than anyone else right now."

"What about you?" I asked.

"I'm not going to leave these people behind," he said. "They don't deserve to die alone. That matters to me. I know it does to you too."

I ruminated, sipping my piss poor coffee.

"What am I supposed to tell my wife?" I asked.

"I can't tell you what to say," he said. "You'll need to find those words yourself."

It took longer to find those words than I imagined. I had sacrificed so much for my profession. I've lost time with my family. I've given up sleep and sanity. You name it, I've gave it up at some point. As Peter Parker's uncle would say, "With great power comes great responsibility." This however, was something I didn't think I had in me to give up. It was all I had left, but these people depended on me to watch over them, until I was unable to do it any longer. I reached for the phone and dialed home.

"I don't understand," Marie said.

That was an understatement. That response came after ten minutes of very tense arguing. She had every right to be angry. I was mad too, at myself mostly for putting them through this.

"I need to stay," I said simply.

"No. You don't. There has to be someone else."

"Marie," I said softly. "There is no one else."

There was silence on the other end of the line. She knew there was nothing to be said that would dissuade me from this.

"I cannot abandon them. I just can't," I said.

"You'll abandon your family?" she said.

"Marie...I..." I started to say but stopped. I was losing focus. I didn't know what to tell her.

"You know what pisses me off the most about this?" I said.

"What?" she asked.

"The fifth floor."

"The fifth floor?"

"Yes," I said. "The fifth floor is the maternity ward. A whole floor of newborns; little boys and girls that won't get to see their first birthday. That angers me greatly."

"I'm sorry," she said.

"I don't want this," I said finally. "I really don't."

"I know," she said. I could hear her crying.

"Tell the kids I love them," I said.

"I will," she replied.

"Marie?"

"Yeah?"

"You're my whole world."

I heard a click and the line went dead.

So this was it. There was no right answer. No matter what I did, I would hate myself, but I made my choice.

I would stay.

Until the end.

Soon enough, there was another code blue. We were able to save this one, for now. She was eight years old, a victim of a serious auto accident. We could only keep her comfortable; there was not much else we could do at this point.

After she was stabilized, everyone left the room but me. The girl reminded me of Angela. My emotional distance was broached once more. I was reminded every day that every patient I dealt with could be just as easily be someone I cared about.

The girl opened her eyes.

"Hey there," I said. "You gave us quite a scare."

"Is this heaven?" she asked.

"Nope, you're still here with us Robin," I replied. "My name is Josh."

"Hi Josh."

"We're going to keep an eye on you and make sure you're going to be comfortable. Okay?" I said.

"Okay," she replied.

"All right then. I have to go do my rounds. I'll check on you later."

"Dr. Josh?" Robin asked.

"Yes?" I replied.

"Does it hurt to die?"

Her question froze me. No eight-year-old should have to ask that question.

"Uhh..." I stammered.

"Tell me," she said.

I racked my brain, searching for the right answer.

"No, it doesn't," I said.

"It doesn't?"

"No, it's like going into a deep sleep. And when you wake up you are surrounded by your family. There's no pain and everything's peaceful."

"You truly believe that?" she asked.

"I do," I said."

"Thank you Dr. Josh."

"You're very welcome Robin. I'll see you soon."

My job made me feel so powerless sometimes, now more than ever.

Saturday afternoon, a silent munity occurred. Half of the staff disappeared without explanation. Now there were only a handful of doctors and nurses in charge of dozens of patients. This couldn't have come at a worst time.

The day continued on. Save a patient, lose a patient. The merry go round of life continued to twirl. All I could do was my job and not ponder things. We still had a few good people left that helped share the load. One of them was Amy, an intern. She was twenty six and she could have been anywhere else, but she stayed on board. Her ability to mind the details in the middle of this madness was astounding. She was greatly appreciated. Needing an answer to a question that had been bothering me, I pulled her aside.

"Amy?" I said.

"Yes?" she said.

"I have to ask you something."

"Of course," she said

"Why did you stay?"

She stewed on the question.

"You know when this first started," she said, "I thought everyone would join together and help each other. We could never do that when things were fine, but I look out there and it only got worse. Then I see people like you. You have a wife and kids. You have every right to go home and spend your last moments with them, but you stayed. You helped these people when no one else would. You do this with no thought to yourself. You're one of the reasons I stayed."

"Thank you." I said.

"No, thank you," she said, before walking off to continue her rounds.

Everything was falling apart, but you wouldn't know it from inside these walls. My people were scared, but they didn't show it. They did their jobs. I've never been more proud of my staff.

Though I didn't see anything in regards to the outside world, radio broadcasts filled me in well enough. Nothing was sacred anymore; morality and common sense were a thing of the past. I understood it on some levels; they could do whatever if there would be no one left to judge them.

These actions were just a waste of time, time that could not be redeemed. If this turned out to be yet another false alarm, they would recoil in horror from what they had done. They would see why we wouldn't deserve to exist. For man is weak and fallible.

If one is deprived of sleep long enough, sooner or later they crash from exhaustion. I was at my breaking point. I needed to rest. I shut my eyes and I was gone.

In the dream I was home.

It was late and I had only small pockets of light to guide my way. I tried to flip on the lights. None of the switches worked. Not a good sign. I walked up the staircase slowly to not wake up the kids. It turns out I didn't have worry, they were already up.

"Daddy! Help me!" Angela screamed.

I bolted up the stairs and burst into her room. She was being dragged out the window, by what I could not ascertain. Her small hands

were gripping the windowsill for dear life. I
held her arms, trying to pull her back. I looked
around to see what had her. There was nothing
there.

"I'm scared, daddy," she said.

"I know, Daddy's got you," I said.

I placed my footing firmly into the wall
and pulled with all my might. I started to bring
her back. However, with every inch I gained,
the entity pulled back more. I could feel her
fingers unlatching from mine.

"I'm losing my grip," she said.

"Hold on Angie, just hold on," I said.

The force yanked back hard and Angela
was dragged away into the black nothing. Her
screams dissipated to nothing.

I called out for her. It was no use. She
was gone.

"Josh," Adam said, shaking me awake.
My eyes came back into focus. I was back in
the hospital.

"How long was I out?" I asked.

"Forty minutes."

"Not long enough," I said.

"Tell me about it. I wish I could let you
sleep. I really do."

"Here," He said, handing me an energy
drink. Those kinds that teenagers chug so
they can play Madden all night. "There's
enough caffeine in this to kill an elephant.
Drink up. You're going to need it."

"Thanks," I said.

I popped the can open and took a large
sip. The energy blend brought me back, just a

little. I would probably be having a few them by the time the day was over.

"We got any patients that need immediate help?" I asked.

"No," he said. "That's not why I woke you up."

"Why then?"

"Marie and the kids are here," he said.

Angela and Tyler rushed me the moment they saw me. I grabbed both of them up in a bear hug. I never felt so happy to see them. I was on the verge of tears. I looked to Marie; her expression was stoic.

"I thought they should see their father," Marie said, "Show how hard he's working."

"Doing a good job Dad?" Tyler asked.

"You know it buddy," I replied.

"Save any people?" Angela asked.

"Lots of them," I said.

I stood up and went over to Marie. I held her in my arms.

"Can we go somewhere and talk?" she asked, "Privately?"

I saw Amy out of the corner of my eye.

"Amy," I called out.

"Yes, Doctor?" Amy said.

"Listen, I know you're busy, but can you watch my kids for a few minutes? I need to speak to my wife."

She nodded. She knew I was saying goodbye.

"Take all the time you need," Amy said.

I pulled Marie into a storage closet where we wouldn't be disturbed. I shut the door and locked it.

"I had to come," Marie said.

"I know," I said.

"I know you didn't make this decision easily. You care so much."

"Perhaps too much," I said.

"Don't apologize," she said. "It's part of why I love you."

"Marie, I—"

She held a finger to my lips and caressed my face.

"No more talking," she said.

"You promise to listen to your mother?" I asked my kids.

"Yes," They said in unison.

"Brush your teeth."

"Yes."

"Say your prayers."

"Yes."

"Be good."

"Yes."

"That's my little rascals," I said, hugging them each one last time.

"When are you coming home Dad?" Tyler asked.

It was clear they had no clue what was going on. It was for the best.

"I'll be home soon, buddy," I lied. "We'll play catch in the yard later okay?"

"Okay," he said.

Marie's face was ash. We knew this could be it.

"I'm still mad at you," she said.

"I know," I replied.

"I'm also proud," she said.

I kissed her. "I love you," I said.

"Same here," she said.

After they left, I found an empty corner and collapsed to the floor. Two days of stress flowed out of me. Amy sat down beside me. She was as stressed as I was.

"I appreciate you watching my kids while I was with Marie."

"No problem," she said. "It's nothing."

"Do you have someone?" I asked. "Someone you need to say goodbye to?"

"You mean like a boyfriend?" she said.

"Yeah," I replied.

"His name is Chad. He actually came by earlier. I had someone cover for me."

"I see."

"Yep."

I laughed for no reason, probably so I'd stop crying. "I need to get back to work," I noted.

"As do I," she said. "Look at it this way. Either way it will all be over soon."

Every second that passed put me more and more at unease. It was an odd feeling, knowing I was only hours away from death; that we all were. I didn't want to leave yet. I wished for things that would no longer be possible.

I had never been a dye in the wool Christian, but I still believed. I closed my eyes and prayed. Prayed that I would see home again, hold my family once more. It might not have done much in the long run to say those prayers, but on the other hand, it couldn't hurt.

Early Sunday morning, there were only a few of us left. I was glad to see Adam and Amy were still there. We were running ragged at this point, trying to keep patients comfortable. I didn't know how much time we had left. No one did.

By mid day there was a lull in the rounds, so I headed up to the fifth floor. The children were mercifully asleep and at peace. For that I envied them. There was one exception. A baby girl was crying at the end of the second row. I picked her up and began rocking her to calm her. I didn't want her to wake the others. The combined crying would have been excruciating.

"It's all right. Everything's all right," I whispered softly. She seemed receptive to my words as she stopped crying almost immediately. I laid her back down into her bed. Her little hand reached up and gripped my finger. I searched her chart for a name.

Alexa.

Alexa Morris.

"Hello Alexa," I said.

Alexa looked up at me with bright blue eyes and smiled the way only a newborn could. It warmed my soul just a little. It that moment, I knew no matter what happened life would prevail. Things were going to be okay.

"Welcome to the world," I said.

TOM

I was the only child to two loving parents that busted their asses to give me opportunities they never had. They worked jobs they hated, with people they couldn't stand. They were young once and probably had dreams different from where they ended up. This was the hand they were dealt and they strived for me never to be in the same situation. All I needed was a little bit of time. Just take the summer off from college to figure out what I wanted. As I found out later, time was a luxury I would no longer have. I would be left with plenty of things undone.

Thursday had started out normally. I was with Kylie, my lone gal pal. We were taking a hike in the woods not far from where we lived. We kept it active whenever we hung out.

"It's hot," I noted.

"Wuss," she said, teasingly.

"Ninety degrees is hot."

"According to you," she said.

"Don't bust my balls."

"Wouldn't want to offend your feminine wiles would we?" she asked coyly.

"Of course," I replied.

The trail turned unexpectedly and my foot got caught on an exposed root from a nearby tree. My body twisted and I hit the ground hard. Sharp jolts of pain ran up my side, but I ignored them. I was just glad I didn't twist my ankle. Kylie, the loyal friend she was, was merciless in ribbing me.

"Gotta watch where you're going," she said, laughing.

"Yeah, yeah," I replied, pulling myself up and dusting off. "Shit happens."

"Only to you apparently; you're a walking klutz Tom."

"You're so nice. No wonder we're friends," I said sarcastically.

"Aww, you know you love me," she said.

You're right Kylie. I do.

I can hear you now. Wow, how original, guy falls for a girl that happens to be a friend of his. No one has ever seen that before. I know how pathetic it looks. Yet the fact remains; I am in love with her.

People always ask the proverbial question; can men and women be friends? Women would say yes. Personally, I would say no. My reasoning being that with the opposite sex, emotions can get twisted. Women are good at compartmentalizing; they can exclude guys as romantic prospects quite easily. It's funny how girls always say they would rather marry their best friend, but never consider it in real life. I can see you don't believe me.

Have you ever noticed a lot of those romantic comedies involve a guy pining after a girl he's friends with? The girl goes after a total jerk and gets burned. The good guy will finally profess his feelings. There will be multiple misunderstandings, before they eventually get together, living happily ever after. Now how many times does that actually happen in real life?

I rest my case.

Kylie and I have known each other since we were kids, so there has always been affection there. My deeper feelings for her only started a few years ago. She was always beautiful; that was a given. It was in the details. She had bright green eyes, the color of granny smith apples. Her brunette hair used to be long and wavy until senior year when she chopped it off for a pixie cut that never seemed to look quite right, but either way she was beautiful to me.

Her physical attributes weren't the only reason I loved her. It was also about who she is. I feel that I could tell her anything (except the one thing I wanted to most). She's easy to be around. I'm genuinely happy when we're together and genuine happiness is in short supply. It never seemed to progress past friendship though. She even broke my heart without even realizing it. She told a group of our classmates that she could never date me, and I was sitting right next to her as she said it. Yeah, that day sucked.

I never gave up. Granted, I didn't let it consume me. I did other things. I dated other girls (albeit to little success). However, I never stopped believing we could be more someday. I never found my courage though, because I was afraid if I told her, I would lose her.

After our hike, I headed off alone to Ian's. Ian is my best friend. I've known him for ten years. He knows my ordeal with Kylie inside and out and feels for me. Ian could never understand why I was never given a fair shake by some girls. He knew I was a decent guy. Ian never had those problems. He was a regular ladies man with seemingly no effort. We could never be more different. My moral code prevented me from doing the things he did, but I still looked up to him. His confidence was something I aspired to have.

At his house, we played video games for an hour, and then switched to Satellite TV. It was late and there wasn't much on considering it was nearing the weekend, the dead zone of television viewing.

"There has to be something on. Something with copious blood flow or tits," Ian said, sighing.

I laughed. The line itself wasn't particularly funny; how he delivered the line was. His mind was always in the gutter. Ian paused on his entertainment search with a Steven Seagal flick.

"How was the hike today?" he asked.

"Good," I said. "I had myself a nice face plant."

"Fail."

"Yep, epic," I said.

Ian sighed again. Something was up.

"What?" I asked.

"Why do you keep torturing yourself spending time with her? You know she'll never see you that way," he said.

I nodded. "I know."

"Then why do you do it? Why do you put yourself through it?"

I'd thought about it before. It would be better if we just stopped being around each other. That would be the logical thing to do, but there is nothing logical when it comes to loving somebody.

"I care about her a lot," I said. "I want her in my life, even if I'm only going to be her friend."

Ian understood. "I get it," he said. "Hell of a toll though."

"It is," I replied. "I like being around her. I wouldn't put up with it if I didn't."

Ian continued scrolling through the listings until he found something he liked.

"Got it," he said, relieved. "Firefly is on Syfy. You up for it?"

"Always, Captain," I said, mock saluting.

Ian clicked the remote and we were immersed in good times. I wish I could tell you we got to stay there.

The episode had five minutes left when the screen went black.

"What the hell?" Ian said, puzzled.

For a moment I thought it could have been a power outage, or the satellite going bad, but we had electricity in every other part of the room. So it couldn't have been that.

The screen kicked back on, but it wasn't Mal and the Firefly crew shooting bandits. It was a bright white screen that stood blank. I now thought the channel was having technical difficulties. I grabbed the remote from Ian and pressed the channel up button several times. We saw different channels but the same white screen. Now I was the one to be curious.

"What the fuck?" I asked.

"My thoughts exactly," he said.

That's when it happened. Letters began to form on the screen. One word became a sentence until there was a short message staring back at us. It spoke volumes. It gave us two critical pieces of information. The world was ending, and we had three days to live.

The networks returned to their normal programming, but that didn't last long. They were quickly preempted by breaking news broadcasts. They spoke of the hijacked signal and what it could mean. Pundits, scientists, and conspiracy theorists shared the screen and talked their heads off.

"What the flying fuck," Ian said.

"Wish I knew," I replied.

"Check the web. It's going to be flooded at this point. News travels fast."

I clicked on Internet Explorer. Ian wasn't kidding. A Google search already showed hundreds of results.

"You're right," I said.

"Told you," he said.

I investigated a few message boards on the subject. The consensus was split right down the middle. The people who derided the claim pointed out that numerous groups in the past had believed to have had indisputable evidence of the world's demise. They had been all proven wrong. How was this announcement any different?

Others believed it was real. If this was a prank, why hadn't anyone taken responsibility? Why the cache of released information? Early analysis showed that the results were too on point to be outright dismissed. Both sides had valid points, but I couldn't make up my mind.

"Tom," Ian said, "Come quick. The President is doing a live press conference."

I returned to the couch and watched the press conference. The President fielded questions from the rabid journalists and took them apparently with an air of control. Yes, they were investigating the hijacked signal. No, they had no leads. No, they would not comment on the validity of the statement. The President then told the nation they had no reason to panic. Everything was going to be fine. He quickly stepped off the podium abruptly while the reporters continued to shout questions to him. The feed returned to the talking heads that proceeded to contextualize what he had and hadn't said.

"Huh," Ian said. "That's government for you. Evasive and giving no straight answers."

"No," I said.

"What do you mean no?"

"We learned a few things, actually."

"Such as?"

"The government usually is evasive when something bad is going on. They know something," I said.

"And what else?" Ian asked.

"He told us not to panic. People are going to do that no matter what. That's not what we should be thinking about. The question isn't whether this is a joke."

"Then what is?" Ian asked.

"What if it's true?" I said soberly.

The words hit Ian hard, for he didn't believe any of it for a second. Now I could see the gears in his mind turning, mapping out the scenarios.

"If that's the case, in the words of Jude Law from *Gattaca*—"he said.

"We need to get drunk immediately," I finished.

Lucky for us, that wouldn't be a problem. Ian's parents were total boozehounds. Not in a destructive sense, but they enjoyed drinking, perhaps a little too much. They had a cabinet stocked to the hilt. We avoided most of it, and went straight for the good stuff. We grabbed some shot glasses and proceeded to get smashed. It did not take long.

We decided to play a game as we drank. Every time we took a shot, we would state something we wanted to before we died. Being inebriated, red blooded teenage males, you can imagine where it went.

"I want to fuck two chicks in the same day," Ian began, his voice already slurring.

I laughed. "I want to watch John Woo movies all day."

"Good answer," he said.

That's how it went for ten shots. We'd say something, clink glasses, and throw them down the hatch. The alcohol made us think this was just another game. We could pretend that it wasn't real.

"Last shot," I said. "I'm close to my limit."

"Okay," Ian said, pouring the rum. "Last wish, make it count."

"You first," I said.

Ian breathed in deep.

"I just want to enjoy what's left, you know?" he said. "Value it. What about you? What do you want Tom?"

I started to say something different, but I stopped myself. I knew what I really wanted, and I had one final chance to make it reality.

"I don't want to be afraid anymore," I said.

"What do you mean?" Ian asked.

"I want to tell Kylie the truth, about how I feel."

That sobered Ian up real quick.

"You serious?" he asked.

"Bet big, win big," I said. "Only way to live right?"

Ian patted me on the shoulder. "Good man," he said.

"Thanks Captain," I replied.

We clinked glasses and felt the burn.

If this was a normal night, I would have been in some serious shit for being drunk. My folks didn't care for once. I think they were just glad that I wasn't murdered on the way home.

"You've heard?" I asked.

"Yes," Dad said.

"Are you okay, honey?" Mom asked.

"As fine as can be," I said.

"What are we going to do David?" Mom asked Dad.

"I don't know about you guys," I said climbing the stairs. "But I'm going to bed. I have things to do tomorrow."

That was a lie. I had no intention of sleeping, at least not yet. The night was still young. I snuck out of my window and dropped to the soft grass below. Thank goodness I hadn't mowed the lawn yet. It gave me a cushion to absorb the fall. A silver lining of the world ending was no longer worrying about chores.

I took a walk around the empty streets. I wanted to get some fresh air to think and work off the alcohol. The sky was clear with the stars out. The silence was not only uncharacteristic, but odd. You think with the world ending, there would be commotion in the streets, but not here. Not a sound to be heard. You could actually hear yourself think. If the whole place wasn't about to be engulfed in flames it would be very appealing indeed.

I was willing to bet a few people were lucky enough to go to bed before the announcement happened. They slept contently, lucky them. They were primed for one hell of a wake-up call.

Breakfast was bad. There was nothing and everything to talk about. What we usually talked about was tripe considering what our reality was. We ate our cereal, and made no sound except for chewing. I had never felt so disconnected from my family. This was the time we needed to come together. Reassure each other. It was the opposite of that. We were pushing each other away.

Dad pulled me aside afterwards. I assumed that he wanted to scold me now for drinking. I was wrong.
"Tom," he said.
"Dad," I replied back.
"I'm not going to lie and say everything will be fine. I'm not sure it will be."
I nodded because that is what I was supposed to do.
"I wish there was some way I could fix this," he said.
"There's not much you can do." I said.
"Yes, there is," he said. "I can tell you to do one thing."
"Which is?" I asked curious.
"You do whatever you want in the next three days, because you might not have another chance."
I nodded in agreement.

I spent the next few hours doing just that. I collected up all my John Woo movies and begun to watch them with a nice big bowl of buttered popcorn. They were his Chinese films, the ones that were actually good. Bullets flew and bodies dropped. It was truly sublime.
I've been asked why I liked these movies so much, including by my disapproving mother. She considered them nothing more than trash. I liked them because

beyond the action set pieces, there are deeper themes at work. Themes like brotherhood, honor, sacrifice, heroism, courage, and love. All of these relate to the real world. I guess I wanted to be like them, a hero. I would be given an opportunity soon enough.

I was lying down, catching some Z's, when my cell rang. I looked at the Caller ID. It was Ian.

"What's up?" I asked.

"Not much dude. Just off making dreams come true," he said.

"Watching a bunch of John Woo movies myself."

"Good. Good," he said. "I got some news."

"Shoot," I said.

"You know Rose Miller? She has the house at the end of the neighborhood?"

"What about her?"

"She's having a party. She's inviting everyone, present company included."

"Sounds like a plan," I said.

"There's more," he said.

"What?"

"I know that Kylie is going."

My heart skipped a beat.

"Ready to pull the trigger, Tom?" he asked.

"You know it, Captain," I replied.

"Good. I'll catch you later."

"Wait," I said.

"What?" he asked.

"What dream came true?" I asked. I knew the answer. I just wanted to him to say it.

"Two chicks. Same day," he said.

"Shut up."

"There's more. Get this; twins."

"Get the fuck out of here," I said.

"And neither knew the other had done the deed."

"You're a total whore. Just saying," I said, laughing.

"I know right?"

We arrived when the party was already in full swing. Alcohol was flowing freely and drugs were being openly consumed. I considered having some, but that was one bridge I swore I'd never cross. The end wasn't going to change that. I'll just stay with liquids.

The music was loud enough I could actually see the walls shake from the vibrations. Partygoers were conversing all around us and it became difficult to think. We pressed forward, searching for an open spot so we could breathe.

I had on a backpack stuffed with liquor we swiped from Ian's house. It was enough to kill several people. It would last fifteen minutes here. No matter, the bag was our passport to one hell of a party. The music was good and the women were gorgeous. I had eyes for only one though. I just had to find her.

I found Kylie in the kitchen, talking to Rose. The conversation involved stilettos and diet cola. Whatever it was, Kylie sure found it amusing. I gave her a tap on the shoulder.

"Hey sexy," I said. Kylie turned around and saw it was me.

"Tom!" she said, wrapping me in a bear hug, "I'm so glad you're here."

"I wouldn't miss it for the world," I said truthfully.

"We got enough alcohol to last till morning," Rose said grinning. "It's going to be a very good night."

"Well, you kids talk," Kylie said. "I need another beer."

"Later," I said. Kylie disappeared into the backyard. I watched her go. When I returned to reality, I saw Rose's face. She wore a bemused expression.

"What?" I asked, wondering what I did.

"I knew it," she said.

"Knew what?"

"You're in love with her."

The air in my lungs locked up. No one knew about that but Ian, and he kept his mouth shut.

"Quit messing around," I said.

"No," Rose said, "I had my suspicions, but it's clear now you are. You're not exactly subtle. Besides, it takes a woman to know. If Kylie wasn't so clueless she would've seen it a long time ago."

I let her response set in for a moment.

"Well, what do I do then?" I asked, finally admitting it to her.

"Well, first things first," Rose began. She reached into a cabinet and pulled out a bottle she had apparently been hiding from the crowd. She spun the top off and poured a generous swath into a red plastic cup. She handed it to me.

"What's this?" I asked.

"Liquid courage," Rose said. "Drink it."

I downed it quickly. The liquor was bitter, drier than I expected. However, I couldn't deny I felt more at ease.

"Now what?" I asked.

"Now you go get her Romeo," Rose said, giving me a wink.

"Rose?"

"Yeah?"

"Why are you helping me?" I asked, puzzled.

"Kylie's a great girl, but she wouldn't know a good guy if she tripped over one," Rose noted, giving a small shrug. "I want to give her a chance at that. Good luck Tom."

I looked for her.

Which was not easy, believe me. If you've ever been to a large party then you know its standing room only. Good luck getting anywhere under those conditions. Out of the corner of my eye, I saw her in the living room, the one place Rose had roped off. I ducked under the barriers and entered.

"Hey," I said. "I've been looking for you."

"You were?" Kylie asked. "Sorry. Had to get some air; even the backyard is crowded."

"I hear that."

"Come on, take a seat. Don't be shy," she said.

I sat down next to her.

"Having a good time?" she asked.

"Yeah, sorta," I replied.

"See any cute girls?"

"One," I said.

"Then why aren't you out there talking to her?"

Let the awkwardness begin.

"I don't know—"I began but Kylie cut me off with a wave of her hand.

"No time to hesitate, literally," she said. "We'll practice, you and me."

"I don't think that's such a good idea," I said.

"Don't be such a sourpuss Tom," she said. "I'll start. Hi, I'm Kylie."

I sighed. "Hi, I'm Tom."

"It's nice to meet you Tom. Tell me something—"

"I love you, Kylie," I said.

Fuck.

Now it was really awkward, but it was also relieving. A large weight had been lifted off of me. I could feel it go.

Kylie did not take it in stride.

"I'm sorry?" she asked, confused.

"I'm in love with you," I stated again.

"Don't play games Tom," she said.

"Does it look like I'm laughing?"

"Stop it."

"Oh for God's sake—"I said before leaning over to kiss her. I took her by surprise, but she seemed receptive, if only for a moment. When we broke away, her eyes were glassy. She looked like she had something to say, but couldn't find the words.

I took a deep breath.

Now or never kid.

She didn't take it well, to put it mildly. Kylie didn't say anything. She just bolted out of the room. I tried to follow her, but she vanished into the crowd which had grown exponentially in the past hour.

I forced my way through the mob searching for her. I looked everywhere, but she was nowhere to be found. I retreated to the kitchen, trying to breathe. The air had become hot and humid with all the bodies smashed together. I felt someone grab my shoulder. I whipped my head around.

"What the hell did you say to her?" Rose asked, concerned.

"The truth," I said.

"Well it turns out that wasn't the best course of action."

"You're the one who told me to be honest," I pointed out.

"I know that," Rose said, exasperated. "I didn't expect her to take it like that though. She grabbed a whole bottle of vodka. You need to find her Tom, before something happens."

I found Ian outside trying to put his best moves on a willing female. I pulled him aside.

"Dude, what the hell?" he said. "Don't cock-block me now. I was about to close."

"Have you seen Kylie?" I asked.

"No I haven't. Why?"

"Well, let's just say she's looking for trouble," I pointed to his cup. "Any beer in that?"

"Yeah," he said.

I grabbed it and chugged it in two gulps.

"What is going on?" Ian asked.

"I took my shot," I said.

"How did it go?"

"It didn't go as planned,

"I'm sorry man."

"I'm not done yet," I said.

"What?" he balked.

"I'm not letting it end like this. I refuse to."

"Tom you got to—"

"I have to make this right, Ian."

Ian nodded. "Then go get her," he said. "Now get lost, I'm trying to get laid."

I finally found her passed out in a chair in the den. Judging by how much of the bottle was missing she was going to have one hell of a hangover. A guy was sitting next to her, trying to cop a feel. I grabbed his hand back and pulled him away from her.

"What the fuck man!" he said.

"I think it's time for you to leave," I said.

"Fuck off, I'm busy."

"I can see that. How about you find a girl that's actually conscious," I said.

"Mind your business, asshole," he said, pushing me away.

I grabbed the son of a bitch by the collar and yanked back hard. He wasn't expecting that. He tumbled to the floor.

"Maybe I didn't make myself clear, so let me spell it out for you. That girl is a friend of mine so whatever you thought about doing isn't gonna happen. You are going to leave now, and if I see you anywhere near her again, I will fucking kill you."

"You're not going to do shit," he spat, hitting me in the face. I wiped it off.

"Look at me," I said giving a cold glare. "Do you want to bet your last twenty four hours on it? You don't know me. You don't know what I'll do."

His frat boy bravado shut down for a moment as his tiny brain ran the variables and realized it wasn't worth it to fight me. His silence signified his response.

"That's what I thought," I said. "Leave."

The guy scrambled back into the crowd of people and I returned my attentions back to Kylie. She was in no condition to go anywhere but home. I scooped her up and began to walk. She lived a good four blocks away from here. This was not going to be fun.

"Come on," I said as if she could hear me. "Let's get you home."

It's exhausting to carry a passed out drunk girl. Not to mention having to constantly reposition her in your arms so you won't drop her. It can tucker out the strongest guy.

Kylie didn't have a key on her, so I didn't have a choice in the matter. I had to ring the doorbell. Her father answered the door. He looked less than pleased.

"Tom? What the hell happened?" he asked.

"She drank too much," I said. He ushered me inside.

I climbed up the stairs and found her bedroom on the right. I placed her down on the bed and flipped the covers over her. Kylie, who had been out cold till now, started to come around

"Where am I?" she asked, her voice raspy.

"Home," I said.

"How did I get here?"

"I made sure you got back safe."

"You're so sweet Tom," she said, snuggling deeper under the covers. That was all it took for her to fall asleep. That was my cue to leave.

Kylie's father was waiting for me at the front door.

"I want to know what happened," he said.

"I told you, she drank too much."

"Don't lie to me son. Something else happened, didn't it," he said.

I had no problem in being honest with him. He just wouldn't like what I had to tell him.

"There was a guy. He tried to take advantage," I said.

He nodded. "You stop him?"

"I told him I'd kill him if he touched her again."

"Good man," he said.

"I meant it," I replied.

"I know you care about her."

"I do," I said, abruptly. "Goodnight, I have to go."

I headed back home. Ian was probably banging a chick by now. More power to him. At least one us would be having a good night. It wasn't going to be me. I had one thing I needed to do, and I messed up.

However, even though I felt like crap, I could die knowing I manned up and told her. Most guys would have let those emotions stay bottled up and they would have suffered for it. At least I didn't have to hide anymore. She finally knew. My mind was clear. I didn't have to take this regret to the grave.

I cannot remember most of Saturday. It went by in a blur. I remember taking a hike alone. I hung out with Ian. We watched a flick, and then I kicked his ass at Halo. We hugged it out like grown men and then I headed home, sobered by the fact that it may have been the last time I would ever see my friend.

Mom made her best roast for dinner. The food seemed to break the tension for a moment. We began to talk again. It was nice. It couldn't last though.

I was about to head up to my room to listen to some music and down some hidden Morgan when a knock at the front door changed my plans. I swung the door open, and there stood Kylie.

"Hi," she said.

"Hey," I said back.

"Kylie," I heard my mother say behind me. "What a nice surprise. Come on in."

I let her in, having no choice in the matter.

"So, what brings you here?" Mom asked.

"I wanted to see if Tom was up for something," Kylie said.

"Like what?" Mom asked.

"I was thinking of doing a night hike," Kylie said. "There's a little bit of ground we haven't covered yet. I have some sleeping bags. I thought we could sleep under the stars."

"That sounds like fun," Mom said. She turned and spoke directly to me. "It's fine by me, though I'd want you back first thing in the morning." Mom then winked at me. I wanted to die right there. Luckily for me, I don't think Kylie noticed.

"All right Mom," I said.

"So, are you game?" Kylie asked.

"I'm game," I said.

We reached the peak at dusk, having to use flashlights to find our way around. We set down sleeping bags and took in the stars. It was quiet, but not exactly by choice. Things were awkward, and she broke the silence first.

"Have you ever considered how insignificant you are?" she asked.

"Wow," I said. "That hurt."

She playfully hit me. "I didn't mean you specifically, silly. Look at it this way. We've know each other for a long time right?"

I nodded. "Since we were kids," I said.

"That's right. Our relationship is important and it has value. However, in the larger scheme of things it means nothing.

What we are primed to lose is minuscule compared to what billions are about to."

"I never thought of it that way before," I said.

"Yep," Kylie said. "Though thinking about that really depressed me. I could use a drink."

"Never fear, my lady," I said, reaching into my bag for the bottle of Morgan I had planned to consume alone. "I have just what the doctor ordered."

Kylie smiled. "My hero," she said.

I filled two glasses. "I'm an ex-boy scout. Be prepared as they say."

A glass or three later, we were feeling pretty good. Not drunk, just nursing a good buzz. We were lying on the ground and I could feel Kylie moving closer to me. I turned on my side to face her.

"We haven't talked about what you said last night," she said.

"I know," I said.

"I'm sorry I freaked out like that."

"I'm sorry I said anything."

"Don't say that," she said. "That took courage. I know it that wasn't easy for you."

"It wasn't," I noted.

"Why did you wait till now?" she asked.

"I was afraid to lose you," I explained. "You might have stopped being my friend. I couldn't risk it. When this happened, I had nothing to lose."

"I would've given you a chance," Kylie said.

"No, you wouldn't," I replied.

"How could you be so sure?"

"Remember that day in English? You told ten witnesses you'd never date me."

Kylie's face went red and she laughed.

"Sorry about that," she said. "Not one of my brighter days."

"You think?" I said, grinning.

We went quiet again, looking at each other. She was going to be the only love of my young life. That was okay. To me, she was perfect. All I would ever need.

"Tom," she said. "I need to say something."

"Okay."

"I can't be friends with you anymore."

My chest tightened up as she spoke the words that I had been dreading.

"Kylie, wait—"

"Tom, I wasn't finished," she said. She moved her index finger in a "come closer" gesture. I moved forward until our faces were mere inches apart. She whispered into my ear, her cool breath tickling my skin.

"I want something more too," she said.

She looked at me and grinned. I kissed her. She offered no resistance this time. I pulled her body close to mine and felt how soft she was. Our lips parted. She smiled; so did I.

"You're a good kisser, Tom," she said.

"Well, with the right person maybe," I said.

"There's not much we can offer each other, with so little time," Kylie said.

"Then tonight will have to do," I said. I nibbled at her neck and slid my hand under her shirt, feeling the warmth of bare skin.

The sun decided to rise right into my eyes. I vainly used my hand to block the rays, but at that point I could not deny it. I was awake, and had to let my eyes focus. The world wasn't scorched yet which was a good sign. Kylie was sleeping next to me. She looked peaceful. It annoyed me greatly to do it, but I had to wake her.

"Kylie," I said quietly, gently nudging her. "It's time to go."

She mumbled incoherently.

"I'm sorry?" I asked, confused.

"Is it morning?" she asked more clearly.

"Afraid so," I said.

"Damn."

"Yep," I said.

We collected our things and found our way down the hill. Kylie and I walked quietly, holding hands. We didn't say a word. We had said everything we needed to the night before.

Kylie and I stood outside her house, stalling the inevitable goodbye.

"So..." I said.

"So..." she said.

"I guess this is it."

"Yeah," she said.

She got closer, arching her feet to reach up and kiss me.

"Thank you for loving me," she said, "You mean everything to me, you know that right?"

"I know," I replied.

She headed for the porch and was almost at the door when I called out one last time.

"Kylie?" I asked.

"Yeah?"

"What are you doing Monday?" I asked.

She wore a sad smile. "Not much actually," she said.

"I'd like to take you out on a date."

"I'd like that," she said.

"Okay," I said. "I'll see you Monday."

She opened the door and disappeared. I stood there for a long time. Eventually I had to move on down the road. I had one last stop to make.

"Get the fuck out of here," Ian said, his jaw dropping.

"Usually that's my line," I deadpanned.

Ian and I were in his room, doing some shots before I had to get home. We had destroyed the liquor cabinet over the past few days but it was of no importance. Not like we could take it with us anyway.

"I'm proud of you man," he said. "Who says geeks don't get the girl?"

I laughed. "Thanks man."

"Bottoms up?"

"Bottoms up," I said.

We clinked glasses one last time.

Near the end, Mom was inconsolable. Dad tried to comfort her and tell it would all be okay. I sat nearby, watching the clock tick.

I thought of Kylie.

Tick.

I thought of Ian.
Tick.
I hope they thought of me too.
Tick.

Made in the USA
Middletown, DE
23 February 2016